A HOMICIDAL MANNER

Third instalment in the Matthias Kork, Investigating Coroner series

A HOMICIDAL MANNER

Coronial crime fiction travelogue

by PETER TINITS MD

Dying Medium Press

Name: Tinits, Peter, author
Title: *A HOMICIDAL MANNER*
Description: A Canadian coroner, investigating a death on a train, gets caught up in international intrigue.
Subject: fiction/medical, crime, mystery and detective
BISAC: FIC035000, FIC050000, FIC022020
ISBN: 9781068901928 (hardcover), 9781068901904 (softcover)

Cover art by Stan Oshima
Operating room illustration by Scott O'Neill
Cover design by Ted Glaszewski

Dedicated to the memory of my life-long friend
Jack Douglas Regan

Interviewer: *Can you forgive?*
Vladimir Putin: *Yes, but not everything.*
Interviewer: *What can't you forgive?*
Vladimir Putin: *Treachery.*

Chapter 1

Vancouver, British Columbia

People will always surprise you. You just don't know who they really are by their appearance. I stopped at the bar in the hotel lobby where a pianist was singing 1960s crooner classics. It wasn't offensive, so I sat down and took out my phone to read.

An older couple was alone on the dance floor. The man was heavy-set with a beefy red face fringed with white hair and an unkempt beard. His rumpled clothing and whiskers made him look like an aging back-woods recluse. The woman was a thin Asian, maybe Korean or Japanese. They approached the pianist with a request. He stopped and thought for a moment. Then, he launched into a song in Italian.

The woman leaned into the man such that she would have fallen on her face if he had stepped away. She slid her right foot down the back of her left calf and they danced a tango, stepping over each other's legs in perfect harmony. Her eyes were closed the entire time, relying on him to lead her. They remained alone on the dance floor and they covered it completely.

When the song ended, an audience that had gathered in the room erupted in applause. The pianist put his fingers to his lips and kissed the air. I got up to leave and several bar patrons who had been watching from the sidelines rushed for my seat. People will always surprise you—or this is another example of how everything is everywhere.

To celebrate our thirtieth wedding anniversary, Katya and I had decided to do a luxury train trip on the Rocky Mountaineer. It was June, so the ice would be melted, revealing the famous cobalt-blue mountain lakes seen on picture postcards, and Katya would be on summer holiday from teaching. We had flown from Toronto to Vancouver and checked into the Pan-Pacific Hotel on the Vancouver waterfront.

I love train travel. You have comfort and space. You can read and relax and chat to exotic people. You are insulated from any disturbance from the outside world while moving through its vistas. No one from work can reach you.

I took the elevator back up to our room. We had a view facing Burrard Sound with sea planes taking off and landing. Ferries churned their way to and from the North Shore with its mansions terraced into spruce-blanketed mountains. Although we had gained time flying west, Katya was already asleep in bed, tired from cycling the sea wall around Stanley Park with thousands of other gawping tourists.

At 7:30 the next morning, everyone who was getting on the Rocky Mountaineer train gathered in the hotel lobby. It looked like mostly elderly couples, travelling while they still could. A company official did a roll call, and I noticed the tango dancers step up to be counted. After that, we lined up and filed onto the bus to the train station.

Katya and I had already done this trip five years earlier, in an east to west direction. The Rocky Mountaineer has a class system separating rich or Gold Passengers from the merely well-to-do Silver Passengers. The Golds have a second-floor, glass-domed restaurant car with white tablecloths. The Silvers have their meals served to them in their seats.

In a fit of false economy, I had purchased silver tickets the first time around. The seats that we were assigned were at the front right of the rail car facing a wall, with the best views always behind us on the left. When I complained, a staff member said I could choose an item worth $200 or less from their luxury gift catalogue of jewellery and train-themed memorabilia.

We were travelling in gold this time and seated on the scenic side. The first day was the prelude. We travelled from Vancouver to Kamloops, still shy of the drama of the Rocky Mountains. The views were nice and the food was exceptional. We ate our meals in shifts, with half of the rail car invited to the dining room at a time. There was a lot of excitement when your section was called.

After breakfast, I wandered down the hall to the platform between rail cars that served as a viewing deck. Lowering the window, I stuck my head out like a dog to sniff the breeze. It smelled of pitch and evergreens. When I pulled my head back, I noticed another passenger waiting his turn behind me. It was the male tango dancer.

"Hey, I noticed you on the dance floor last night," I said. "That was a beautiful performance."

"Thanks." His accent was American Midwest. He might have been in his early seventies.

"Are you professionals?"

"It's just a hobby."

"Is this your first time travelling through the Canadian Rockies?"

"Yes. I've been to Canada before—to Toronto and Niagara Falls."

"Congrats." These places were overly familiar to me.

"What about you?" he asked. "First time in the Rockies?"

"I've skied Banff a couple of times and also did a ski package that combined Jasper and Banff with a self-drive on the Icefields

Parkway. The Rockies are the prettiest part of Canada. You should do the Icefields Parkway between Jasper and Banff. I drove it in a winter storm, which was an experience." As a crap dancer, I was trying too hard to impress him.

"Done a lot of travelling, have you," he said gruffly.

"Yes. If I had to guess, I'd say you were ex-military."

"It's a good guess."

"Where did you serve?"

"I was in Vietnam and Iraq."

"So, you were a career soldier? What was your rank?"

"It's not important. I've been retired for over ten years. Tell me where else you've been."

I told him that I'd travelled around the world with a backpack in my twenties after medical school. He said that now that he was retired, he just travelled. He kept his belongings in a storage locker. I didn't ask where his wife kept her belongings or if she was happy being homeless. We agreed that we should have a meal together in the dining car sometime.

On my way back to my seat, I heard snippets of conversation in French, German and Russian. The latter surprised me, as I thought, in light of Putin's attempts to reconstruct the Soviet empire, Russian nationals were banned from mixing with polite society. Katya and I watched the passing scenery. I had the aisle seat, so I tried to tune in on the conversation of the couple seated across from us.

The man was wearing pressed tan-coloured khakis, polished brown shoes with latticed leather tops and a dress shirt. The woman's dark-blue dress was equally conservative and refined. They were probably ten years older than us.

"What language are they speaking?" Katya had noticed I was eavesdropping.

"I can't tell. They're speaking very quietly," I said very quietly.

4

"Don't bother them," Katya said. "You're suddenly so interested in everyone when we're on holidays and start cross examining people."

"It's my job to determine the facts."

I listened some more, waiting for an opportunity to strike up a conversation if they spoke a language I recognized, but it didn't come up. They didn't meet my gaze and it seemed impertinent to address them directly if they didn't speak English.

Chapter 2

Rocky Mountains

A t lunch, Katya and I were seated across the table from an airline pilot, Laurent, and his flight attendant wife, Celeste. He was tanned with chiselled features and she was a mature natural beauty. They both looked to be in their fifties. My cross examination elicited that they were on their honeymoon. He had found and married the woman he should have married the first time around. They had dated 20 years before, but had both married someone else.

He had been living with regret ever since. His first wife had died of breast cancer, and Celeste's husband had left her for another man. Laurent discovered that she was newly single from her Facebook page. It is rare in this life of tangled webs to be able to move up-weave to try a different strand.

I reciprocated by sharing part of our history with our new friends. Katya was in her last year of university and I had just gotten my medical licence. I am three years older than her. I had seen her coming and going with different boyfriends, but didn't know her. We were living in the same six-plex building in Toronto.

Before specializing, I briefly worked at the walk-in clinic on campus. I was busy perusing new patient charts, which were stacked

6

in a tray at the front desk. She was standing at the head of a line that wasn't moving because she was holding it up, looking at me and smiling.

She had blonde shoulder-length Cleopatra-style hair with bangs cut straight across. She was tall, five feet ten, with freckled cheeks, wearing a simple summer dress. I felt her stare and said, "I sense that you want to tell me something."

"Yes?"

"That you like me?"

"Yes."

"Could we see each other more often then?"

"Yes." She was nodding and laughing.

Impulsively, I put my arms around her slender waist and we kissed. She formed her smiling lips into a semi-pucker that was still a smile. The kiss lasted only a second, and then we were standing smiling at each other again before I had to go back to work.

"You have to take care of the girl going into cubicle three," I said to the other doctor on duty at the clinic. "She can't be my patient. We're about to become romantically involved."

They seemed entertained by my story and nodded approvingly. I had been genuinely moved by theirs. Celeste said, "Merveilleux. Thank you for sharing, Matthieu."

Searching through my vocabulary, I responded, "Merci à vous d'avoir partagé," which I hoped meant the same thing.

We pulled into Kamloops at 7 p.m. The train was parking for the night so that we could traverse the Rocky Mountains in daylight. Kamloops is a hot, dry cow town at the confluence of the North and South Thompson Rivers. We dropped our bags off at our hotel and I went for a run, discovering The Noble Pig Restaurant. It celebrated an alternative to cow meat for our dinner. It. In the morning, we were back at the train station for day two.

Since we had been called second on day one, our end of the rail car was called first for breakfast in the upstairs restaurant. I saw that the tango-dancing couple was sitting alone at a table. He might love blindly following orders and military bravado. Nevertheless, I asked if we could join them because they seemed unusual. When they didn't refuse, we slid in beside them.

He was wearing the same or similar clothing to yesterday. The white hair and beard around his boozy face had had a cursory combing. She was better composed in a pink floral-print sundress.

"Newlyweds?" I asked. "Most people here are newlyweds or nearly-deads."

"No," the man laughed. "We've been together for five years."

"I'm Matt. This is Katya. We're ahead of you in years together. Hopefully, you won't catch up."

"Hopefully," he echoed. "We're John and Hana."

"Hello," Katya said.

"Very pleased to meet you," Hana said in a soft, high-pitched voice. Her smile was warm and engaging, and revealed small pearly-white teeth. Her eyes telegraphed intelligence, and devotion when she looked at John. Although she might have aged very well, she appeared to be more than a decade younger than him.

We studied our menus. I said, "You mentioned that you're ex-military."

"Yes. What about you?"

"I'm a coroner and an anesthesiologist." I said coroner first so I wouldn't have to launch into a discussion about corpses.

"You must have seen a lot of corpses."

"Yes. I presume you've seen some."

"Yes."

"So, Hana! How are you enjoying the trip so far?" Katya interrupted.

"So lovely," Hana said. "Being here is such a privilege. So spiritual. Matthew, you looked like a policeman when I saw you in Vancouver, so serious and tall with your black baseball hat and sunglasses. Now you look more like a doctor."

"My father and grandfather were policemen," I said. "When I travel to a different city, cops will sometimes nod to me fraternally."

"Katya, I think you are a teacher. You have a kind face and so wise."

"Thank you, Hana! I *am* a high school teacher, on summer vacation."

Hana was perspicacious and Katya has a kind face because it naturally reflects her personality. When the waitress came, I was third in sequence to order, after the two women. "Can I order two things?" I asked.

"Certainly sir. You can order as many as you like."

"I'll have the eggs benedict, a side order of toast and the fruit yoghurt granola parfait." That might have been three things.

"Me too," John said emphatically.

"Are you coming to Lake Louise and Banff with the tour?" I asked.

"We're taking the VIA Pan-Canadian train from Jasper across the country," John said. "I like trains and we live on the train line."

"Where?"

His wife looked at him. John said, "East of here."

No shit, Sherlock. They were keeping secrets from me. "I thought you lived out of a storage unit."

"We're going back to our unit to restock."

"Out of curiosity, why do you keep a storage unit in Canada?"

"I've always liked Canada and Canadians. You allowed American draft dodgers to find refuge here."

"So, you're not a 'regular army' type?"

"No. After Korea, all America's wars have been discretionary."

"But you made a career of it."

"Yes. I was in for 30 years."

"Were you initially drafted or did you volunteer?"

The food arrived and the conversation took a pause. I was being intrusive, but I was truly interested in his story. John seemed to gather strength from the food. When we had finished, I posed my last question again.

He said, "I was drafted to go to Vietnam but volunteered twice for additional training, in the sniper and then the Green Beret corps, hoping to avoid active duty. When the war didn't end, I was trapped."

Everyone around the table was waiting for him to continue.

"That sounds dangerous," I encouraged him.

"I've been in battles with 90 per cent casualty rates."

I let the horror of that sink in and then asked, "Do you think you survived because statistically someone had to, or because of some special skill you possess?"

"I decided not to die in that jungle. I reacted to every situation swiftly and decisively. I didn't feel any remorse until I got home." He was becoming agitated as he spoke. His jaw muscles were tense and his face was getting redder.

"He got the Medal of Honor and the Purple Heart," Hana said.

"They were consolation prizes for staying alive," John said.

John had also served in Japan and Iraq, although not in combat. I was impressed by and felt uneasy with his fierce melancholy. His attitude absolved me from having to say thank you for your service. When the meal was over, Hana said that they didn't share these stories with many people.

Travellers on long train trips will tell you things they would never ordinarily tell a stranger. Maybe because time seems limitless and you expect never to meet again. I remember thinking that I would prefer to have this man on my side when teams are being chosen for armed combat.

We hurried back to our seats to watch the main event, the passage through the Canadian Rockies. When we approached Mount Robson, the highest peak, the tour guide announced that we were extremely lucky. As the weather was clear, we would have a full view of its snow-capped summit, which only happened twelve days in a year. Everyone rushed to the Mount Robson side of the train to take pictures. We gasped and rushed to the opposite side as the train chugged along the shore of Moose Lake, which was extraordinarily long, blue and rimmed with mountains and evergreens.

Chapter 3

Jasper, Alberta

The train trip ended in Jasper. We lugged our luggage 15 minutes by foot to our hotel. The tour itinerary allotted two days here, which we planned to spend hiking and sight-seeing. The sun was setting when we chose a restaurant amongst the many that specialized in buffalo burgers and beers. The next morning found us on the main street in a shop that sold outdoor gear. When I asked about bear spray, the clerk showed us a canister that cost $50.

"What do you think?" I asked Katya.

"It looks okay. Seems expensive, hon. Maybe we don't need it."

"I think we should get it and keep it in my backpack just in case, hon." We said hon and darling, not as endearments, but to tease each other. We felt we were above such plebeian norms of behaviour.

"Oh, that won't be quick enough," the clerk said. "You need to keep it on your belt."

I was now absolutely sold. "Like a gun in a holster. Do you sell holsters?"

"Right this way, sir."

"And some bear bells?"

"Over here." He showed us a rack full of various types.

"Do you know how to recognize bear poop in the woods?" Katya said. "The poop is mixed with bear bells."

We had grilled cheese in a trendy diner and rented mountain bikes after lunch. Cycling away from the town, I was thinking about how close I would let a bear get before discharging the spray. We had gone several kilometres through dense forest with bells a-jingling when we stumbled upon Jasper Park Lodge, where we had stayed on the previous trip. There were some deer on the trails but no carnivorous man-eating predators.

The Lodge is one of the grand, historic Canadian Pacific Railway hotels. They were built to popularize train travel after the trans-national railway was completed to unite the country and deter American expansionism. Most of them were named Chateau something. The chain was purchased by a Saudi Arabian company in 2006, which our forefathers did not foresee, and rebranded as Fairmont. After Jasper, our tour itinerary promised all Fairmonts, with the expense hidden in the overall cost of our package.

On day two, we rented a car and drove to Maligne Lake for the ferry ride to Spirit Island. I noticed many of the passengers from the train in the boat with us. We docked after travelling a half hour along the narrow glacial lake. Everyone was snapping pictures of the tiny verdant island with a stand of evergreens, surrounded by cerulean water, jutting shorelines and mountains kissed by wisps of cloud.

I walked along the shore to find a camera angle excluding every human being before snapping my shot. Returning to Katya's side, I said, "This has to be one of the most beautiful spots on earth." I noticed a reverential tone in my voice.

On the ferry ride back, I was standing beside a short plump woman with black curly hair. "You were on the Rocky Mountaineer train with us, weren't you?"

"Yes," she said tersely.

"Everyone here is celebrating an anniversary or a wedding. Did you misplace your husband?"

"Don't worry. I have had husbands." She had a slight accent, maybe Slavic.

"That's right. Why would you want another? After a certain age, they don't add value to a woman's life. You don't need one."

She seemed to value my insights because she smiled and followed us along the hiking trail when we got off the boat. "I'm Matthew. This is Katya," I said.

"I'm Svetlana. Very nice to meet you."

"Thank you," I said. "What nationality are you, Svetlana?"

"I'm American."

She wasn't native-born American. I decided to temporarily respect her privacy if she preferred not to say. "Where do you live?"

"I live in New York."

"Brighton Beach?" This was the Russian area.

"Close to there," she said.

"How are you liking Jasper?"

"Typical," she said.

"What do you mean?"

"Typical mountain tourist town."

I found that pretty harsh, or she was compensating for an inferiority complex. "You must have done a lot of travelling."

When we were out of earshot on the trail, I said, "Russian internet bride who married an American and then dumped him after three years when she got citizenship."

Katya said, "She was taking pictures of the tango dancers while everyone else was taking pictures of Spirit Island."

"What do you mean? Why would she be doing that?"

"She was doing it unobtrusively and quickly."

"Well, maybe she likes the tango."

In the afternoon, we drove the short distance from Jasper to Whistlers Mountain. Besides my wife, there was only one other passenger waiting for the gondola. It was a middle-aged guy wearing a Harley-Davidson jacket. He was about six feet tall, solid-looking like a rugby player, short brown hair, cleft chin, unshaven. He had classic, underwear-model good looks turned scruffy.

We boarded together. It was very quiet in the cabin. "First time to the Rockies?" I asked.

"Nah," he said.

After a minute, I offered, "It's strange that they built this imposing gondola, but there are no ski trails. It's just for sightseeing."

"I was in the Rockies as a ski bum 20 years ago, mate." His accent was Australian or New Zealand.

"Aussie, Aussie, Aussie," I said to draw him out. It was a football chant. The response was *Oi, Oi, Oi.*

"Too right, mate."

I held out my hand. "Hi. I'm Matt. This is Katya."

He accepted the handshake. "Jack Rielly."

If you give them the opportunity, with a little prompting, people will quickly tell you what's top of mind. Jack was separated from his wife. He was tragically responsible for the death of his 13-year-old son, who was riding as a passenger on the back of his motorcycle. He was driving too fast. They hit some gravel on a curve and skidded out. His son suffered a lethal head injury. Jack's wife couldn't forgive him. He revealed all this in the space of five minutes.

He had decided to quit his job and take a trip across the Pacific to lose himself. My heart went out to him. He looked grizzled and defeated. There would be no going back and starting over. He was too old to meet, court, be engaged to and marry someone in time to make another son.

It had nearly happened to me. I was dog sledding with my son Michael in rural Quebec. The guide had given us hasty instructions.

The driver stands at the back of the sled and the passenger sits just in front of the driver. He told us the French words for stop and go, how to steer and how to engage the brake, a blade at the back that dug vertically into the snow. We should only give commands or praise to Bijou, the lead dog.

Taking first turn as driver, I stood as Michael sat ahead of me, covered by a blanket. Soon after we set off, the dogs got into the spirit of the thing, running at full tilt down a narrow trail, shitting and pissing on the fly. The left runner of the sled rode up onto a snow bank. The brake waved uselessly in the air because instead of digging into snow, it was elevated off the ground, digging into nothing. I was thrown off the sled as it was being dragged on its side.

I screamed, "Bijou arrête!" but Bijou didn't obey. Seeing that my son's head was on a collision course with a tree trunk, I tried shouting at Michael to duck as his head snapped back ever so slightly. I saw my life flash before my eyes and walls of regret and remorse. I was wailing in my head: *if only I could roll back time… if only I was given a second chance…* I don't know how it is possible, but Michael was uninjured. He had no memory of hitting the tree and there was no mark on him.

My guardian angel was stronger than Jack's. Without its timely intervention, my life might have unfolded as Jack's had. I wanted to tell him that I was sorry and knew how he must feel, but there were no words sufficient to express this. I wanted to tell him that we could hang out and be friends, but it was too early.

"Did you rent a bike here?" I asked.

"I'm on a train-bus tour that ends up in Calgary. They call it the Rocky Mountaineer."

"Hey, we're doing the same thing now that Katya's on holiday from teaching high school. See how ecstatic she looks?"

Katya obligingly flashed some teeth. "How have you found the tour, Jack?"

"It's good. Great views. Nice people." He pronounced *people* like *pay-pull*. These people were celebrating honeymoons and wedding anniversaries, which would make him feel his losses more acutely.

"Average age a little older than you?" I asked.

"Yeh," he grunted. "Good teeth though."

"Old and rich. VIA Rail is cheaper but it goes at night. There's no other way to see the mountains by train in daylight," I said.

"I'm taking the VIA train the rest of the way to Toronto. Always liked trains. You can't see the sights if you're steering a car."

Or a motorcycle, I thought. "How long does the trip take?"

"Three days, more or less, I reckon."

"Are you coming to Lake Louise tomorrow?"

"On the Icefields Parkway. Should be good." He didn't smile or look excited.

"I'm terribly sorry for your loss. You did the right thing in coming to Canada." I actually reached over and gave him a hug.

The gondola ride ended above the tree line. We got off together, but I lost sight of him in the crowd waiting to ride back down. Katya and I hiked over shale rubble almost to the top of Whistlers Mountain. We turned back because of high winds that were whipping rain in our faces. When we reached the gondola station, they had closed the lift because of the weather.

We were stuck at the top waiting for the wind to subside. There was a restaurant perched on a precipice overlooking a picturesque, sheer drop where we had an overpriced meal. I searched the room but didn't see Jack anywhere. I was worried he might have sat down on the mountain side, to await death in the storm, or thrown himself off a cliff. When the gondola re-opened two hours later, there was still no sign of him.

The next morning, I went to look for coffee and croissants while Katya got ready for our trip to Lake Louise. There were no more lavish, free breakfasts as we had enjoyed on the train. I met Svetlana in the hotel lobby. "Good morning, fellow tourist," I said.

She looked at me wryly. "Yes. Good morning. Where are you going?"

"I'm off on a breakfast run, looking for some fancy coffee. What about you?"

"I will come."

It didn't take long to find what I was looking for. Svetlana followed me into a bakery, where they had some fresh loaves of dense, dark rye bread out for sampling. She came over holding a piece out to me. "I took too much," she said.

"Thanks. This is the kind of bread I ate growing up."

"It would be very good with some vodka."

"That is Russians' answer for everything," I said.

She looked at me accusingly. "There is nothing better to take for a cold. Or for indigestion." She was serious.

"Or for a heart attack or a hangover."

"So, you know."

We walked back together carrying our cappuccinos and pastries. When I entered the room, Katya had her suitcase packed and was styling and blow-drying her hair.

"I met our friend Svetlana again, hon," I said.

"Did you ferret out whether she's a Russian agent?"

"Judging by her love of rye bread and vodka, she's Russian. If she came on a tourist visa prior to the fall of communism in 1991, she would have had to have left a husband or children behind. She wouldn't have been allowed out as a single woman. She would have been interviewed by the KGB before leaving and may have been given an errand."

"Did you tell her that after he left the police force your father worked at Radio Liberty broadcasting Western propaganda to the commies?"

"That would have been provokatsiya."

We joined a group of Rocky Mountaineers gathered on the curb outside the hotel waiting for the bus to Lake Louise. Everyone had specialty coffees to enhance the experience and ward off the morning chill. With a couple of sightseeing stops, the trip would take about five hours. It was a thinner crowd than before as some people had made alternate plans. Svetlana was standing off by herself.

Chapter 4

Lake Louise, Alberta

Walking down the aisle of the bus, we said hi to Svetlana as we passed her sitting alone. The bus stopped at Athabasca Falls beside a collection of several other tour buses. Exiting with Katya, I lifted the corners of my mouth at Svetlana and we walked together along the path to the falls.

"Katya's of Polish extraction. Her parents were Polish," I said. "My parents were German and Estonian. What's your background, Svetlana?"

"Yes. I have been to Estonia. They think they are European somehow," she said.

I was astounded. Soviet Russia forcibly incorporated Estonia into the Soviet Union, and modern Russia looks at Estonia the same way as it does Ukraine. I said, "They are undoubtedly European, as is all of Russia west of the Ural Mountains."

"Yes. They think they are better than us."

"Not better, just distinct, and independent."

She shrugged.

"Did you marry an American, Svetlana?"

"Of course."

"How did that happen?"

"it's a very long story."

"You don't feel like sharing? That's okay, but I will tell you my secrets if you tell me yours."

"No. It is not interesting."

"Do you like tango dancing, Svetlana?"

"No."

As we were walking, she fell a step behind us. I noticed Jack, the Aussie from our gondola ride, coming toward us on the path. So, he hadn't ended it all. I rushed forward to greet him. "Guddeye, mate!"

"Guddeye," he said back.

"I was wondering what happened to you. I didn't see you on our bus this morning."

"We're on a Brewster bus. I don't recognize anybody from the train. It seems to be open to everyone now."

"Well, it's great to see you again. I lost track of you at the top of Whistlers Mountain."

"Thanks mate. Had a walk round. It was a bit blustery. Nothing to hang onto up there."

"Us too. It was really windy. They closed the gondola so we had dinner up there. I'm glad to be back at ground level."

"I must have caught the last one back before that. Well, that's me, mate. They're waving our group back onto the bus."

"Wait. What's your next stop? Maybe it's the same as ours."

"Not sure. I reckon they're all the same. See you down the road then." He walked back to the queue that was forming outside one of the buses.

I reluctantly followed his progress until he boarded. "He's a definite suicide risk," I said to Katya. "Recently bereaved, marital breakup, male, no support group…"

"Do you think we could contact him to stay in touch?"

"I didn't get his contact information. The opportunity didn't come up."

"Maybe you'll see him again."

Our second stop was at the Athabasca Glacier. We boarded an elevated all-wheel-drive bus, designed to drive on ice. It ground along slowly over the terrain into the middle of a snow field, where we got out to walk around. It was picturesque, but I'd seen snow before. One of these buses had capsized in 2020, killing three people. I didn't see Jack there.

Lake Louise is a Canadian classic. It used to be featured on the back of our ten-dollar bill. As soon as our bus pulled into the parking lot, the passengers disgorged and fanned out around the perimeter of the lake to marvel at the bluest of blue waters ringed by snowy peaks.

Historic, grand and opulent are appropriate adjectives for the Chateau Lake Louise Hotel, with its high ceilings and solid-wood doors that swell with humidity. The charm is magnified because it is the only hotel on the lake. It is situated in Banff National Park, where development has been halted. We had stayed here once before, but familiarity did nothing to diminish the majesty.

We went up to our room to check out the view. It was the same full panorama as on the currency. Our luggage hadn't arrived yet, but we were wearing our hiking boots. We set out to hike the path around the lake. There were still traces of snow on the evergreen boughs. The moisture gave off a pungent Christmassy fragrance. It reminded me of the old Salem cigarette commercial claiming that a puff was a lungful of springtime in the Rockies.

Off in the distance, I saw a familiar figure walking toward us, dressed in a spandex T-shirt and carrying a motorcycle jacket slung over his shoulder.

"Hey Jack, old friend. Are you staying here? How was your walk? Do you want to do dinner together tonight? Maybe we can throw some shrimps on the barbie."

"Yeh, all right."

"This is great," I said. "I'm in my element." I made a sweeping gesture with my hand.

He didn't say anything.

"We stayed here 20 years ago. It hasn't changed at all. And we did après-ski drinks in the lounge here après skiing Lake Louise a few years ago. It has this great view through high-arched windows. We should do dinner there."

I saw him smile for the first time.

I took out my phone. "Give me your cell number."

"Yeh, all right. Here it is then." He recited the number and I entered it into my contacts.

I gave him another man hug and said, "See you tonight then."

When he was out of earshot, Katya said, "You've really taken a liking to him. You don't normally hug anyone."

"I lost a good friend to suicide after a marital breakup. You remember Luke. This is just as bad. He reminds me of Luke and a few others."

After our luggage arrived in our room, we suited up and took a trip to the pool and the gym. Katya was wearing the complimentary hotel bathrobe, which seemed too informal to be worn in public, but she knows more about propriety than I.

At 6 p.m., I texted Jack to ask if he was hungry yet and we arranged to meet in the lobby bar. They did the same food as the hotel restaurant at a surprisingly reasonable price. We ordered spicy tuna bowls and two extra hamburgers in case it wasn't enough food.

"So, Jack, what do you do in Oz?" Katya asked.

I wondered whether this was wise. He was, after all, trying to get away from memories of home.

"I was a dentist, Katya. I had a surgery in Sydney, which I sold to a dental corporation."

He was even more of a suicide risk if he was a dentist. They have the highest suicide rate of any profession.

"Sydney is a beautiful city," Katya said. "They've kept development from closing off the waterfront to pedestrians. I loved the paths from the Botanical Gardens and Opera House to the seaside boardwalk with the shops and restaurants. It's all high-rise condominium towers in Toronto. You wouldn't think convicts would care about such things."

She was teasing him, but he wasn't taking the bait.

"Convicts are harder to bully," I said.

"You've been to Australia then, Katya?" Jack asked.

"Yes. We were on a cruise. There were volunteer seniors in red shirts at all the points of interest giving directions to tourists. And Matthew was there another time before that."

"After medical school," I said. "I did my house surgeon year in Auckland, New Zealand—the equivalent of a Canadian internship. Cars and gasoline were expensive, so I learned to drive a motorcycle. After it was done, I toured Australia by motorcycle with an Australian guy who I trained with."

"What did you think of Australia then?" Jack asked.

"An unpretentious, hot, dry Canada built by convicts."

"We're not all convicts, Matthew."

"No, probably not." A vignette about Australia came to mind. "I was stuck in traffic on my bike on an Australian highway in 30-degree heat, and a guy in a silver Mercedes beside me lowered his window. He beckoned me over and poured me a cup of ice-cold water from a thermos. It went down like a charm. He reached in his wallet, wordlessly offered me a five-dollar bill through the window and then closed it again. It was the strangest thing."

"Did you accept?" Jack asked.

"Of course. He was rich and I was sweltering. He couldn't invite me into his car."

"Five dollars was worth ten dollars then. No wonder you like Australians," Katya said. "Did you like being a dentist, Jack?"

24

"I don't know. I was good at it, but nobody's happy to see a dentist. My undergraduate degree at uni was in physics. Dentists are paid better than physicists, if they can find a job at all."

"Is there nationally subsidized dental care in Australia?"

"No, and there is no official fee schedule. Unscrupulous practitioners can charge whatever they can get away with. About half of people have private dental insurance through their work. People do dental tourism in Bali or Bangkok if they need major work and want a cheaper price. I felt uncomfortable charging people for dental care if they couldn't afford it."

"I'm sure you were very ethical in your dealings," Katya said.

"I tried to be Katya, but the corporation I sold to isn't known for that."

Jack must have sold to Drillum, Fillum and Billum. They also have offices in Canada. I noticed that Jack tossed a ten-dollar tip on the table for his share of the meal. Aussies are known for categorically refusing to tip based on the theory that everyone is equal. It might have been my story, or because dentists are well-off and therefore more equal.

Returning to our room, we crossed paths with Svetlana again, looking in the hotel shop windows. She was a little curt with her greeting, and I was afraid that perhaps I'd upset her. She said that Lake Louise reminded her of many other places that she had already visited.

She couldn't help being Russian and having persecution and inferiority complexes. Russia was populated by people in her predicament. One benefit of Putin's special military operation against Ukraine was that most of them were currently barred from travelling to the west.

In the morning, we boarded a bus that took us to Emerald Lake and then on to Banff. The Banff Springs Hotel is a glorious castle. It has a spectacular setting nestled on a promontory overlooking the

Bow River Gorge and Falls, two kilometres from the town. Having been built in stages, it has a labyrinthine variety of corridors and lounges. I walked around the hotel with my Kindle and notebook for writing down good ideas, looking for the best place to sit and read. It had to have the optimal compromise between mountain or river view and quiet.

All the couches by the windows in the lobbies were already occupied. All the seats in the library were taken by elderly card sharks and board game players. Eventually, I found a lounge off the beaten path with some empty seats. Naturally, the window seats were taken, but I ensconced myself comfortably in the middle of the room in an armchair, feet up on another chair, notebook and Kindle on my lap.

Feeling a bit fatigued, I put the items on the table beside me, took off my glasses and lowered my eyelids.

After a few minutes, I looked up, feeling someone staring at me. The older gentleman, who had sat across the aisle from me on the train, was standing beside me. In accented English, he said, "You look like an intelligent man. May I ask you a question?" He was tall and aristocratic-looking, wearing his pressed khakis and brown brogues.

I felt that he had hit the nail on the head. "Thanks for the compliment. What can I do for you?"

"Why would an intelligent man such as yourself put his feet up on that chair?"

The attack was totally unexpected. I was wearing sandals and had been careful that only the heels and not the soles should touch the cushion in front. I looked around the room. There were still some vacant seats, so I wasn't depriving anyone of a place to sit. Without removing my feet from the chair, I said, "I'm very comfortable. Does that bother you?"

26

"It is not proper behaviour. What if everyone did that?" His accent was German.

"It's acceptable behaviour where I come from. Everyone does it."

"I don't believe this. Where do you come from?"

"Canada. I don't believe that your countrymen have historically set a very good example of proper behaviour."

He glared at me. I could have said it in German, but I didn't want to tip my hand.

I saw that Katya had entered the room, and not having noticed me, was about to sit down. I called her over, removed my feet from the chair and insisted that she sit on it. This was to show the German guy how much Canadians loved to sit on chairs that had been until only recently occupied by clean sandals.

"Excuse me, but is this your wife?"

"Yes," I said, expecting another angle of attack.

"There was another woman who passed just here by and picked up your book and spectacles."

I groped over the side table and found only my Kindle. My notebook and glasses were gone. I felt suddenly angry. The glasses cost $800 and some of my best ideas about things to see, do and read were in that notebook. "Who did you say picked them up? Was it an employee?"

"She was a short lady with dark curly hair."

"Which way did she go? Is she here now?"

"No. She went here out." He pointed to the hallway I had come by.

"Vielen dank." Thanks a lot.

"Also, Sie sind Deutscher. Das hab' ich gedacht. Oder Sie sprechen ziemlich gut Deutsch." He thought my German pronunciation was too good for me not to be German.

"Estnisch. Ich hab' Deutsch studiert." I told him I was Estonian. It's easier to learn a foreign language if you already speak one.

"Also, Baltendeutscher." Okay, you're Baltic German then.

"Vater Estnisch, Mutter Baltendeutsche, in Kanada geboren." Father Estonian, mother Baltic German, born in Canada.

He bowed and walked back to his chair.

"What did he say?" Katya asked.

"He said that Svetlana stole my notebook and glasses."

Katya had a hard time keeping up as I rushed down the rabbit warren of hallways looking for the reception desk. I got the attention of the woman behind the counter and asked, "Did anyone turn in a pair of glasses and a notebook to you just now?"

"No sir."

"Do you have a lost and found?"

"Yes sir. Housekeeping can check it for you."

"Do you have a woman named Svetlana registered with the Rocky Mountaineer tour group? I don't know her room number. We were supposed to have dinner together."

"I'm sorry sir. I can't give out information about other guests. I could contact her and ask whether she would like to call you. What is your room number?"

I took the little cardboard jacket that held my key card out of my pocket and read the number off. She brought the guest registry up on her computer and said, "I'm sorry sir. There is no one named Svetlana registered with your tour group."

"Was Svetlana on the Rocky Mountaineer with us, Katya? Do you remember?" I asked.

"I don't know. Let me think. I don't think I saw her."

"Can you tell me whether there is anyone named Svetlana staying at the hotel?" I asked the clerk.

"There is no one by that name currently registered at the hotel, Doctor." She must have seen the *DR* before my name on her computer screen from the VISA imprint they took for incidentals and decided to be more helpful.

She paged housekeeping and I waited around while they checked. My lost belongings weren't in the lost and found. Luckily, I had a spare pair of glasses in my luggage. There are benefits to having an anal personality.

"Why would she do that?" I asked Katya. "Does she think she needs my glasses to decode the secret writing in my notebook?"

"I don't know," Katya said.

The dinner menu prices at the Banff Springs were of course outrageous. At any rate, we wanted to see the town. When Jack texted me, *What time for shrimps on the barbie, mate*, I suggested that we catch the bus to town and look for Happy Meals there.

Chapter 5

Banff, Alberta

There was a bus that ran into the city every 20 minutes. We met in the hotel lobby and, following instructions from the receptionist, walked to the end of the circular drive to catch it. The bus dropped us off on Banff Avenue, the main drag.

We found a pub that was full of college kids. They worked in the resort hotels in summer waiting for the ski hills to open, when they also operated lifts and sold hot chocolate. It was a sign that the food here would be more affordable. The odour of burnt charcoal ushered us in.

"You buy a new pair of glasses, mate?" Jack asked after we were seated.

"I don't know whether you saw her. There was a Russian woman on our tour with dark curly hair who filched my other pair."

"Took them off your face, did she?"

"From a table while I was having a nap. I have a witness. She seems to not be staying at our hotel anymore."

"That's strange. She would have no use for them. Did she seem malicious or larcenous?"

"She seemed like a typical Russian."

We perused our menus. "Sorry, there's no kangaroo meat on the menu, Jack," Katya said, "but Alberta is renowned for its beef."

"Alberta burger and a beer then."

"Burgers and beers all round?" I suggested.

"A zero-alcohol beer for me," Katya said. "Alcohol gives me nausea, crawling skin and hot flashes now."

"She used to drink all the time, didn't you, hon. She can't drink at all now. She's like a pregnant alcoholic."

When the food arrived, Katya picked up her burger, took a bite and held it aloft like a trophy. "Happy anniversary, darling!" It was June 28, our wedding anniversary.

"Happy anniversary, hon." I leaned over and kissed her greasy, puckered, waiting lips.

"How many is that then?" Jack asked.

"Just thirty," Katya said.

"We've been together longer than we've been apart," I said.

"Congratulations…" There was an awkward pause. Then Jack said, "I've tried to make sense of the accident and why my marriage broke up. I'm near enough to being a good person. I can only blame myself for my carelessness. It was my carelessness, my speeding that killed my son."

In a quiet voice, Katya said, "It was an accident, Jack. You can't foresee every circumstance. Life is a series of accidents. Have you seen the film *Sliding Doors*? Two completely different versions of Gwynneth Paltrow's life result from whether she gets on a subway train or misses it by a few seconds."

"It was a Ducati, the Rolls Royce of motorcycles. It wasn't the first accident I've had. I won't get on a bike again. I love riding, but I sold it. If I had never bought it, my son would still be alive. The day that I bought it was the day that I set the sequence of events in motion that led to his death."

He wasn't wrong. Motorcycles are dangerous. In the hospital we call them sui-cycles, or donor-cycles. They result in more donor organs becoming available. I didn't tell my son this when he was a teenager, but if he had ever expressed an interest in buying a motorcycle, I would immediately have bought him a car.

"I had three motorcycle accidents during my year in New Zealand," I said. "I did a U-turn not far from the interns' residence in Auckland, ended up instinctively driving on the right side of the road, hit a car head on merging from a highway off-ramp, flew over it and landed on my feet like a circus acrobat. As I was dragging my damaged bike home, a police car stopped to ask what had happened.

"I related the series of unfortunate events to the policeman. Despite the lack of witnesses or property damage to anyone else, and based on my own statement, they sent me a summons in the mail charging me with careless driving. My last day in New Zealand was two weeks before my court date. I mailed the summons back from the airport with a note saying that I would not be appearing to contest the charges."

"You're an escaped fugitive but never a convict, mate." Jack said.

I said, "Here's what I know. On a macroscopic level, things are determined. The sun will exhaust its fuel in five billion years and all life on earth will disappear. Events are more random on a microscopic level. Subatomic particles wink in and out of existence and their positions can only be described in terms of probabilities. Your accident was a tragic random event."

"Thanks Matt. I know you're trying to help. You're a friend."

"Do you think there is any chance of reconciliation with your wife?" Katya asked.

"No. She hates me."

"Do you have any other children?"

"No. I have two nieces."

32

"I don't want to be glib," I said, "but at least there will be some remnant of you left behind when you are gone."

"I've thought about putting a gun in my mouth. Luckily, they're difficult to find in Australia."

"Please don't say that or think that, Jack," Katya said. "I know that you're in pain. You don't want to cause more grief for your family. It's hard to believe now, but the passage of time will dull your pain. The fact that you are here in the mountains means that you can still appreciate that there is beauty in the world."

"I know that, Katya. I don't know whether I want to see it or whether I am worthy of seeing it. I want to live in the alternate universe where this never happened."

"There is a version of you, Jack, where that is true," I said. "You are the version confined to this universe. Please make lemonade out of the lemons served to you here."

On the following morning, there were no breakfast alternatives other than the Banff Springs Restaurant, so that's where we went. I'm not a morning eater, but Katya needs to have breakfast. After a waitress seated us, Katya went directly to the buffet. I noticed the German and his wife seated at another table. As usual, he was impeccably dressed, as was his wife. He looked away with distaste when he saw me coming.

I smiled and said, "Entschuldigen Sie bitte. Thanks for telling me about my glasses and notebook yesterday."

"Did you get them back?" he asked.

"No. I looked around the hotel for the person you described. I'm pretty sure I met her earlier on the tour. She's a Russian, living in New Jersey. I don't know what could have motivated her."

"Sit down for a moment. What is your name?"

"Okay, thanks. Ich heisse Matthias Kork."

"Sehr erfreut. Matthias, before I retired, I was the deutsher Generalkonsul in Moskau. Naturally, we had an apartment in

Moscow in a very nice building. On some days, when we came home, the paintings on the walls were tilted just a bit to one side. On other days, the contents of the refrigerator would be rearranged."

"Is Moscow prone to earthquakes?"

"No. On one day, the alarm clock was missing. One month later, it was back on the table beside the bed. Do you know what I am saying?"

"No."

"The Russian intelligence service, the FSB, was playing games. Their intent is just to let me know that I am vulnerable. You are Estnisch, and perhaps she wanted to show you this."

"Do you think she was a Russian intelligence operative. Why would she care about me?"

"I don't know, but this was my experience in Moskau."

"Thanks for telling me. May I ask your name."

"Max und Hildegard von Scheffel."

"Pleased to meet you. Enjoy the rest of your trip. Where do you go next?"

"We are of course going to take the other Rocky Mountaineer train from Banff through the Rockies west to Vancouver. You too?"

"No. That's way too expensive. One way is close to $10,000. We go to Calgary and then fly home."

"Gute Reise, Herr Kork."

"Danke. Und Sie auch." I got up. He got up and we shook hands.

When I got back to our table, Katya asked, "What were you talking about with the German dude?"

"He seems to like me now. He says Svetlana was playing mind games with me. Maybe I pissed her off. He's the former German Consul General to Russia."

"Well, it's good she didn't poison you."

This was the second last day of our vacation. Our package included a bus tour of Banff and surrounds. As we were leaving the city, the tour guide pointed out the local hospital through the bus window. I knew that the hospital specialized in broken legs and arms from the ski hills and venereal disease. Banff is the venereal disease capital of Canada.

We left for Calgary by bus the next day, a 90-minute drive. It was sad to see the mountains diminish and then disappear behind us. We were still travelling in style though. The bus dropped us at the Fairmont Palliser Hotel, our third consecutive Canadian Pacific hotel—easy to get used to. They always had a terry-cloth bathrobe for Katya, a gym and pool for me. There was someone tinkling the ivories in the lobby when we checked in.

Katya and I did a walk through Calgary's outdoor pedestrian mall. The downtown didn't seem to have much else to offer. The streets would be full of cowboy-hat-toting tourists when the Calgary Stampede rodeo started in a week. I arranged to meet Jack Rielly in our hotel gym and asked him where he was going next.

"I was thinking of taking the train from Calgary east as far as Toronto."

"There is no passenger train going east from Calgary, only a freight train," I informed him. "You could take a bus to Edmonton and catch the VIA train from there, but it's a four-hour journey. To be honest with you, from Edmonton, all you see from the train are endless flatlands and farms going east for two days, followed by endless rocks, trees and lakes for two days in northern Ontario. I think you'd get sick of it."

"Have you done the train trip?"

"No, but I think it would be like that. Why don't you skip that part and fly to Toronto with us tomorrow? We have a spare bedroom. You could stay with us. I could show you Toronto and Ottawa, and Niagara Falls of course. I still have a week off before I go back to work at the hospital."

"You might find it hard to believe, but I think I would actually enjoy seeing that part of Canada. We don't have boreal forest in Australia."

"What if I threw in a jar of Vegemite to sweeten the deal?"

"Very persuasive," he said in an appeasing tone, "but I can't leave out a big chunk of the country like that."

"Okay, well then. I've got another idea. Take the VIA train from Edmonton as you had planned and get off in Coventry, where I live. It's one stop before Toronto. Text me when you know what day you'll be arriving and we can hang out."

Katya and I were packing our belongings in our room for the morning flight to Toronto. She was finished before me and was sitting on the corner of the bed reading the fine print on the ticket. "Hey Matt. Did you know you're not allowed to take bear spray on the airplane, even in your luggage?"

"I'll just take it and won't tell anyone. If you hadn't happened to read the ticket, I would have done that anyway."

"It's a metal canister. It'll show up when they X-ray your bag."

"They don't X-ray luggage, do they?"

"I think they might. It's pressurized. What if it explodes in the cargo hold?"

"Well, it cost $50. I'm not just going to throw it away."

"You could give it to the concierge to donate to some guest who is going camping."

I picked up my phone and texted Jack, *Do you want some bear spray? We can't take it on the plane. Might come in handy if you get off the train to pee.*

He texted back, *Yeh all right. Give it back to you in Coventry.*

Chapter 6

We rose at 6 a.m. to get to the Calgary airport two hours before our flight. The cab had an airport flat rate, so the ride was direct and quick. The seats that I had reserved on the Air Canada flight to Toronto were mid-plane in case the nose or the tail fell off. I had the longest legs, so I got the aisle. Katya was in the middle.

Whenever I heard someone coughing, I put on my N-95 face mask. Whenever they stopped, I took it off. The Covid pandemic had been over for a few years, but I was still gun-shy. A young woman arrived at the last minute to disturb our privacy and apologetically occupied the window seat. At least she wouldn't be getting up to pee every hour like some old man with a prostate.

I was still in holiday mode. "Going on, or returning from vacation?" I asked expansively, leaning across Katya. She gave me a look which telegraphed, leave the poor person alone.

"Oh, hi! I'm flying home to visit my parents."

"Do you work in Calgary?"

"I've been working at the Banff Springs Hotel for six months."

"We stayed there for two nights," I said. "It's gorgeous. Did you find a pair of glasses?"

Our conversation was interrupted before it could blossom by an announcement: *We request any doctors or other medical personnel on board to please come to the front of the plane and identify yourself to one of the flight crew.*

This happened often enough when I was flying. The airlines were too cheap to pay for their own medical staff on board. I usually sank low into my seat and counted slowly to ten before responding when this happened. It left time for a more motivated good Samaritan to come forward. Luckily, I hadn't told the girl in the window seat what I did for a living.

Having reached ten, I put on my face mask and reluctantly got up to have a look. There were two flight attendants and a man and a woman passenger clustered around a seat near the front. The female passenger was on bended knee, holding the hand of a distressed, pale looking woman in her seventies, asking her questions.

"What's your name, dear?" the younger woman asked.

"Anastasia. I'm just so dizzy and nauseous."

"Are you a doctor?" an attendant asked me.

"Yes," I said.

Both of the volunteer passengers stepped back, as one was a firefighter and the other a nurse. I had trumped their credentials. The attendant reached into an overhead compartment and pulled out a tackle box. She snapped a plastic lock off the latch and pushed it toward me. "Here's our medical equipment, Doctor."

Weak and dizzy is the commonest presenting complaint for old people in any emergency department. It is the bane of emergency physicians because it is so non-specific. It could be anything.

"Is it worse when you stand up?" I asked.

"Yes."

The attendants had already cleared the passenger out of the adjoining seat. I took Anastasia's temperature, pulse and blood pressure, which were a little high, a little high and a little low respectively.

Moving the arm rests out of the way, I said, "Let's get you lying down with your feet up then." Raising the legs has the effect of an auto-transfusion. I listened to her chest and squeezed her belly. I rechecked her pulse and blood pressure, which were now more normal.

"Are you on blood pressure pills?"

"Yes."

"Chest pain, palpitations or shortness of breath?" Heart and lung conditions are the most potentially serious causes of weak and dizzy.

"No."

"Can you move all four limbs normally?"

"Yes. I've vomited twice and had diarrhea."

So, not likely a stroke. The combination of dehydration and antihypertensive pills could account for her symptoms. "What did you have for breakfast?"

"I had an egg sandwich from a vending machine."

Today was Monday, so the sandwich had probably been made on Friday. "It may be food poisoning from the sandwich, but it's probably gastroenteritis. Almost all gastroenteritis is viral. There's no specific treatment for either condition. I could start an IV to give her some fluids, but she doesn't seem too bad. Let's try some clear fluids by mouth and Gravol first. Are you okay with that, Anastasia?"

"Yes," she said weakly.

"I'll check on her again later."

When I returned to my seat, both ladies had their earbuds in and were watching screens. I told Katya it wasn't serious, probably just gastro, and tried to doze off.

"Sorry for bothering you, Doctor. Our doctor on the ground wants to speak with you," the flight attendant whispered in my ear. She handed me a satellite phone.

The doctor was from MedER, a private, for profit, telephone consultation company that Air Canada must have contracted with. Pre-pandemic, MedER was a company employing mostly foreign medical graduates that turned everything into house-calls to inflate their billings.

I explained the situation to the doctor on the phone. I had a background in emergency medicine and anesthesiology. Her abdomen was soft. The patient was stable and in no danger. They didn't have to land the plane.

Thirty minutes later, the air hostess woke me up once more. "Our doctor wants you to check Anastasia's vital signs again."

I grudgingly complied. Anastasia was doing better. Her vital signs were fine. I reported my findings to the MedER doctor on the ground. On my way back to my seat, I overheard an older, maskless passenger self-righteously saying to her companion, "…told me to self isolate. For God's sakes, all I had was a little sniffle." Back at my seat, I told Katya to put on her N-95 face mask.

Thirty minutes later, the flight attendant was back with instructions from their doctor for me to check Anastasia's vital signs again. I was getting more than a little annoyed. I had said she was fine. My qualifications exceeded those of the dumbass doctor on the ground. They weren't paying me for my services or for repeated exposure to a mild case of Covid.

I complied but put some pique in my voice when I spoke into the satellite phone. "I told you that she's fine. There's a nurse on board if you want someone to do vital signs every thirty minutes."

When we landed, Anastasia was helped off the plane by two paramedics and then wheeled away on a stretcher.

"Do you think she'll be all right?" Katya asked.

"Yes," I said. "Do your Covid test in a few days."

The drive home from the airport was initially hectic, with speeding drivers not allowing cars from the on-ramps to the highway to merge and transport trucks weaving in and out of lanes. As we got out of Toronto, the traffic thinned and manners improved. I was glad to see farms and forests again.

Our son Michael and his girlfriend Harper had generously been looking after our dog. Their apartment was on the way home. We exited early off the highway and Katya texted him when we were parked outside. They lived on the second floor of a locked house with no doorbell. On the upside, there were no canvassers but, on the downside, no children at Halloween.

Madame Fifi, our Bichon Frise, was of course ecstatic to see us. She had given us up for lost. Michael remarked on my unfamiliar glasses. I told him they were an old pair and that the Russians were using my regular glasses to decrypt entries in my journal. They gave us cups of herbal tea and gluten-free cookies. Katya and I did a show and tell for them swiping through pictures on our phones.

After about twenty minutes, I noticed their attention wandering and that they possibly exchanged a look, so I brought the show to an end. When it came time to leave, the dog was confused and some-what reluctant to accompany us. Michael and Harper had let her sleep between them on their bed, which we would never. Lie down with dogs, wake up with fleas.

I texted Jack from home the next day. *How's the trip going? Are you on the VIA train to Toronto?*

Yes. Arriving in Coventry Thursday July 3. Will you be home?

Yes. I've got Thursday and Friday off to show you around. What time is the train scheduled to arrive?

Arriving 11:33 a.m. but running late today.

Okay. I'll pick you up. Text me when you're getting close.

VIA trains are frequently late. If you ask any of the staff why they're running late, they moan that it's not their fault. They run on tracks owned by freight companies that give priority to freight trains. It never seems to be a problem in Germany or Switzerland.

41

I had my phone turned off, but it was still in my hand when a new text arrived. It was from Zach White, the Chief of Anesthesia, at Coventry General: *Hi Matt. Saw your wife at the supermarket today. I know you're officially off this week. Trying to get staff to run an extra room tomorrow for a cancer case that was postponed. Everything is lined up. Just need an anesthesiologist. Are you able to help out?*

I actually had nothing pressing and he had played the cancer card, so it was hard to refuse. I typed okay and paused to reconsider when he texted, *It's just one case.* His phone must have detected that I was composing a response. I pressed send.

Katya was in the kitchen unpacking groceries. I went in to help unpack and take inventory of what there was to eat. I asked, "Did you see Zach at the supermarket?"

"Yes, he was there. I was going to say hello, but he pretended not to see me."

"He's the generation below us, so he doesn't find us that interesting."

"Women older than age 45 are invisible to men," Katya said.

"Not to their husbands, although it may be familiarity or fear rather than lust that makes them notice."

"Gee thanks."

"President Jimmy Carter never stopped having lust in his heart. He was a gentleman."

Chapter 7

Coventry, Ontario

Returning to work at the hospital the following morning, I presented my badge to the card reader at the entrance to the operating suite. Magically, the doors swung wide to admit me. I changed into my O.R. greens and strolled into the waiting area to interview my patient. He was having a cystectomy and ileal conduit for bladder cancer. This was a biggish six-hour operation to remove the urinary bladder and divert the urine flow to the abdominal wall.

Ruth Faircroft was the urologist doing the operation. The practice of urology deals with maladies of the penis, testicles, prostate, bladder and kidneys. About half of gynecologists are men, but it's rare to find a female urologist. Apparently, men like operating on women's genitals more than women do men's.

As I entered my operating room, I saw by the wall clock that it was 7:35 a.m. This left me a comfortable 25 minutes to sign out my narcotic drugs from the dispensing machine, check my equipment and gas machine and draw up the drugs for the first case. I dropped my bag containing reading material and incomplete coroner files on the floor beside the gas machine. I was planning to use the hours during the second half of the procedure, when nothing dangerous was happening, to catch up on reading and writing reports.

Zach White appeared in the doorway. "Thanks for coming in, Matt. Can you take a med student?" The student was standing beside him, trying to look lovable. He looked older than the average medical student, taller than me, maybe six feet four, with short, dark hair and thick dark eyebrows.

I wanted to say no. The student would be staring at me while I was rushing to get ready, unqualified to help in any way, making me late if I took the time to explain anything to him. On the other hand, by saying no, I wouldn't be setting a very good example, and the rejection might irreparably bruise his sense of self-worth. He had paid his tuition and deserved some value for money. But then again, if I accepted, I would have to spend my day reciting elementary concepts, unable to do any of the other work that I had planned.

My delay in answering prompted Zach to say, "I had him yesterday and I'm doing a list of total joint replacements today." All of Zach's cases would be done with freezing, which required precise positioning of needles beside nerves. The student wouldn't be allowed to participate.

"What year is he in?" I asked.

"Fourth year, his last year of med school," Zach said, selling him enthusiastically. "He wants to practice intubating."

Of course he did. That meant legal liability for me. He might bruise the patient's airway, or instead of putting the endotracheal tube into the windpipe to facilitate breathing, put it in the esophagus or make a new passageway altogether. I reluctantly said, "Okay, come in. What's your name?"

"Thanks," Zach said and vanished.

"Robert," the student said.

"Robert, just stand off to one side while I get ready. You can watch the induction. If we start late, the surgeon will be pissy for the rest of the day. We can talk once the case is underway."

"Okay, sure."

His large solid form was looming just behind me to my left. "Do you know yet what you want to do after you graduate?" I asked.

"I was thinking anesthesiology."

This was supposed to warm my heart. I couldn't tell if he was trying to ingratiate himself or was being truthful. The circulating nurse Sara brought the patient into the room and looked Robert over. We attached the patient to the standard monitors, and I invited Robert to participate. Sara guided him through what to put where.

Ruth Faircroft entered and did a presurgical pause where she recited what she planned to do, and we all agreed that we had no concerns about her doing it.

"Thanks for coming in, Matt. This won't take the whole day, so I added a really short case to follow."

Being fee for service, I would get paid for doing an extra case, but she was abusing my hospitality. I said, "We'll see how this case goes. I'll stay if we can finish by 3:30. That's 3:30 p.m."

"So, who's this you've got with you, Matt?" Ruth was recently divorced and eyed Robert speculatively.

"Robert, the visiting medical student."

"Are you interested in anesthesiology, Robert?" she asked.

"Oh yes. Either urology or anesthesiology."

I got the anesthetic underway and then put a central venous line into the internal jugular vein of the patient's neck. This was to have an intravenous line capable of delivering larger volumes of blood in a hurry than could be managed with an arm intravenous. It was just a precaution. I advanced the catheter tip into the superior vena cava just above the heart.

Robert seemed impressed. "Cool. That's what I want to learn to do."

"You'll do lots of them if you go into anesthesia. Anesthesiologists are the experts in putting in central lines."

"Matt is the line king." Ruth said *line* to sound like *lion*.

I sat Robert down on the anesthesiologist's chair beside the gas machine. "I'm going to get you to do the charting, Robert, and tell you what to write down, so you know what's important. You can ask any questions when that's finished."

I dictated the names of the anesthetic induction drugs and the doses I had given. "Fentanyl, propofol, rocuronium. We routinely paralyze patients with rocuronium for intubation and to provide better operating conditions for abdominal surgery. Do you know the name of the chemical transmitter between nerve and muscle?"

"Acetylcholine."

"Where else is it the neurotransmitter?"

"In the autonomic or involuntary nervous system, for parasympathetic nerves."

"What do the parasympathetic nerves innervate?"

"Heart, lungs, bowel, bladder."

"Right. The sympathetic nerves innervate the same organs but have effects opposite to the parasympathetic nerves. The sympathetic nerves speed up the heart, the parasympathetic slow it down."

"Right," Robert said. He was eager to please.

"Do you know how rocuronium works, Robert?"

"It competitively blocks acetylcholine at the neuromuscular junction."

I was surprised at how much he knew. "Yes. The reversal agent for the paralysis is neostigmine. It is a cholinesterase inhibitor, so it increases the amount of acetylcholine and overcomes the effect of the rocuronium. Cholinesterase inhibitors are also widely used as

46

insecticides. A big dose floods their neuromuscular junctions with acetylcholine, which also causes paralysis, killing them."

"They're also military nerve agents," Robert said. "Too little acetylcholine and too much acetylcholine both cause paralysis."

"Yes." I was warming to Robert. "We use a nerve stimulator to determine whether a patient is paralyzed. It's in the lower drawer of the gas machine. Take it out."

Robert fished a hand-held device with two dangling wires out of the drawer. I attached two sticky electrodes to the skin of the patient's forearm over the course of the ulnar nerve and clipped the wires to them. "It delivers a current like a Taser. Now, press this button and tell me what you see."

"Nothing."

"Right. That means he's paralyzed. After we give neostigmine to reverse the paralysis, he'll have strong twitch responses to consecutive electrical impulses. Neostigmine has to be combined with atropine because neostigmine also affects all the parasympathetic nerve endings in the body. That includes heart, lungs, bowel, bladder. Atropine blocks the effects on those organs. What do you think would happen if we didn't add atropine?"

"The heart would slow—and the bronchi would constrict?"

"Right. You've really done your homework. The heart would slow, maybe stop. Also, increased lung secretions and bowel motility. What did you do before you went into medicine, Robert?"

"I'm a captain in the armed forces. They're paying for my medical school."

Ruth looked up, suddenly interested. "Come around and look at this, Robert. I push this trocar through the abdominal wall. There's a little resistance and then it just pops in like a bad boy."

"Cool."

"Are you married, Rob?" she asked.

"I haven't found the right woman yet."

47

"It's good to be choosy," she said.

When we had finished the charting, Robert asked me, "What do you like most about being an anesthesiologist?"

"It's nice that you're portable. You don't have any overhead. There's a lot of night work though, and when the surgeon calls you, you have to run because everything is an emergency, a command performance. If I had it to do over again, I probably wouldn't choose it."

"What would you choose?"

"Radiology, or dermatology. There is no night work in either of those. There is no night work in pathology, but that's mostly looking down microscopes at surgical specimens. I didn't get the gold medal in my medical school class, so I wouldn't have gotten into dermatology. Radiology, I guess."

"Robbie, an internist, a surgeon and a pathologist go duck hunting," Ruth said. "They spy a bird on the shore. The surgeon asks, 'Is that a duck?' The internist says, 'It swims like a duck. It quacks like a duck. But the differential diagnosis includes goose, swan, heron, tern, peacock and stork. We need to do more investigations.' Blam! Blam! The surgeon shoots the bird dead. He says to the pathologist, 'Now, tell me what it is.' "

I said, "The pathologist retrieves the bird, a bald eagle, pitches it to the surgeon and says, 'Great shot,' to stroke her ego."

Ruth cackled. "Good one, Matt. It's funny because it's true. How do you tell a urologist from an anesthesiologist?"

I hadn't heard this one. "Okay, how?"

"When they're in the O.R. together, the urologist has her hand on someone else's wiener. Ha, ha, ha! I love that joke."

"I want to do procedures," Robert said, "not make lists of differential diagnoses like internists do."

That was my hint to let him do the intubation for the next case. "Okay Robert. You can intubate the next patient. You've earned it." That wouldn't be for four hours.

"Robbie, why don't you scrub in," Ruth said. "I'll let you do some suturing. Matt won't be doing anything interesting for hours."

"Really? Okay." Robert left the room to scrub.

"Are you trying to steal my student?" I asked.

"Holy crap, Matt, he's cute!"

For the next several hours, Ruth and Robert got on like a house on fire. She let him cut and tie sutures, and he expressed admiration for her surgical skill. I was able to fulfil my aspiration of typing out coroner's reports. When Robert took off his mask between cases, I saw that his prognathic, cleft chin already had a five o'clock shadow. Ruth's add-on case didn't require intubation, so Robert was out of luck.

Chapter 8

Returning to holiday mode, I slept until 9:30 the next morning. I wasn't ready to get up, but I had set my alarm to prevent me from sleeping forever. Katya was already up and opening curtains to let in the day.

"I've been asleep ten hours," I said.

"You need your sleep, hon. You're still catching up from ten years ago. And you've been taking call so long that you've confused your on-off switch."

My phone was in the charger by my bedside with the ringer turned off. I saw that Jack had texted me to say that he would be arriving in Coventry at 11:00 a.m. on Thursday if they stayed on schedule. I texted back, *Great, see you tomorrow and text me when you arrive.* Since I lived ten minutes drive from the train station, I wouldn't need much notice.

"Got any plans today?" I asked Katya.

"No. Just more laundry from the trip."

"No book club, movie club, mahjong club, golf club or buck n' doe?" Katya had an active social life.

"Buck n' doe," she said. "Never heard of that until we moved here." It was a fund raiser for engaged couples, peculiar to country folk in our area.

"You bring a sack of toonies, and they provide the raffles, roulette wheels and Timbits. A fair exchange."

"Jack's arriving tomorrow, isn't he?" Katya asked. "Have you made any plans?"

"I was thinking to just show him around Coventry on Thursday. He'll probably want to go to Toronto on Friday. I'd rather just go to the beach in Bayfield. We'll also have to do Niagara Falls."

"Everyone wants to go to Niagara Falls. They're not happy otherwise."

"Do you remember when Lembitu was visiting from Estonia?" I asked, "and he said, 'I thought it would be higher.' "

"Yes. That was disheartening… Eighth wonder of the world."

"I know, right? I'm going to drive in on the Niagara Parkway. That's really impressive. We could do the theatre in Niagara-on-the-Lake in the evening. I'll check what's playing and whether there are tickets."

I spent the day googling things to do in Southern Ontario and going to the supermarket to restock and replace the items that had turned green in our fridge. I settled on coconut shrimp, hummus, grape and paté appetizers to make him feel appreciated, and a nice piece of fatty Atlantic salmon to make him feel the wonder of travel to distant oceans.

I had booked off the week from the hospital but hadn't booked off from the coroners' service longer than our trip out west. They called so infrequently and I could continue to do cremation certificates, which paid $75 each, if I was available. I was about to be punished for my avarice.

On Thursday, as I was getting in my car at 10:45 a.m., my phone rang. It was the coroners' answering service. "Hello Doctor. Can you take a case in Coventry?"

"Can you get someone else? I'm meeting a friend at the train station."

"The other coroner in your area is away. It's a death on board a train at the Coventry train station. You're based in Coventry, aren't you?"

"Yes." This was unfamiliar territory. It wouldn't be an easy or quick case.

"There is no one else available. They want to get the train moving again. Would you like the information, Doctor?"

The Coroners' Answering Service always called when I had something planned. A thousand thoughts raced through my mind. I had no idea how long I could hold up a train or whether I was allowed to formally seize a train. "Okay, give it to me. Is the body still on the train?"

"Yes, as far as I know. It's a VIA Rail passenger train at the station at 47 Railway Drive, Coventry. The investigating officer is a Sergeant Branko Marcovic. Would you like me to spell that for you?"

"No. I know him."

"He's on scene. You can reach him at 519-4372257. The decedent's surname is Sato, spelled S-A-T-O, first name Hana, common spelling. Date of birth 4 December 1975. There's some confusion as to what happened to her. There is a second injured person, sent to hospital."

"Was it a train accident? How long has the train been there?"

"Yes, it's been held up at the station. I don't know how long it's been there. You'd best get down there as soon as you can."

After going back into the house, I asked Katya if she could follow me to the train station in her car and bring Jack home. She didn't look too happy about it but agreed.

I brought up the electronic medical record for the Province of Ontario on my computer. There was one listing with the surname Sato, but the date of birth didn't match. The dispatcher might have gotten the date of birth or the spelling of the name wrong, as they commonly did. I wasn't allowed to access random medical records and I was wasting time. If she wasn't Canadian, she wouldn't be there.

I dialled the policeman's number. "Hi Branko. It's Matt. I got a message to call you about a death of a train passenger. What's happened?"

"Hi Matt. It's a 49-year-old woman, found in her sleeper compartment. Her husband has been sent to the hospital. It might be food poisoning or maybe an overdose. There was an altercation between the husband and another man on the train. At least two others got involved. We're still interviewing witnesses."

"Is there any evidence of trauma?"

"No. EMS was here and pronounced her. She's lying slumped over on the seat in her cabin. We haven't touched her."

"I couldn't find any information about her in the provincial medical database. Give me the name and date of birth again to see if I got it right."

Branko repeated the information, and it was correct on my page. "She's Japanese," he said.

"Oh, okay. Did you get any information about what happened from the husband?"

"He was unconscious when we got here. Apparently, he was one of several people who were fighting in a different section of the train, in a passenger car, when the train pulled into the station. One of them discharged bear spray at the other. We'll have more information when you get here. Don't waste any time. People are whining and the train conductor wants to get moving."

I rang off and hesitated between calling my Regional Supervisor now about the procedure for delaying a train or from the scene. He would probably want more information, so I checked that I had spare face masks and disposable gloves in my coroner bag, completed the toe tag with the decedent's name and set off in my car.

Katya followed me to the train station in her car and we parked in the lot. There were three police cars parked out front and a lot of people in the waiting room and on the platform. I presumed that they were delayed passengers.

"What's going on, Matthew?" Katya asked.

"I don't know. Can you please just wait here a few minutes until I call you? I'm going to go look for Jack. Keep your phone on."

"Okay, but don't just leave me standing here. I'm going home if I don't hear from you."

"Okay. I'll give you Jack's cell number. If you don't hear from me in ten minutes, please give him a call and drive him home. I'll join you as soon as I can."

Katya looked unhappy but didn't object. She stood on the sidewalk outside the station with her phone in her hand. Observing the vestiges of Covid precautions, I donned a mask and gloves from my coroner bag and approached an unmasked, uniformed constable on the railway platform.

"Hi. I'm the coroner, Dr. Kork. Detective Marcovic called me. Do you know where he is?"

"Yeah, he's expecting you. He's inside the train. I'll take you in."

We climbed up some folding steps into a sleeper car. Two men were standing, talking, halfway down the hall. I recognized one of them. He was tall and thin with a hook nose that looked like it had been broken and left to heal.

"Hi Branko. This is different. What have you got?"

"Hi Matt. Were you on holiday? I haven't seen you for the last few cases. You remember Hunter." Branko indicated his companion.

"Hi. I was on a train holiday through the Rockies."

"I want to do that some day. She's inside the compartment. The report I get is that the husband's still unconscious. I would say they both took something, but the husband attacked another passenger sitting in the coach car with pepper spray, so it doesn't look like a suicide pact. Do you think it could be food poisoning?"

"Is anyone else on the train sick?"

"I haven't heard of anyone else. As a precaution, I instructed my men not to go into the compartment in case there's some new ultrapotent narcotic shit like carfentanil on her clothes or in the air."

"I'm wearing an N-95 mask and gloves. Hopefully, that's enough," I said. "When was she last seen alive?"

"A French-Canadian couple who had the compartment across the hall discovered her. They said she had looked unwell after coming back from breakfast. They checked on her half an hour later and found her dead."

"Do the combatants know anything about what happened to her?"

"Well, we can't find the guy who was attacked with the spray. An Australian guy, seated in coach, got up to intervene and was himself attacked. I'm wondering if it's some kind of domestic love triangle drama. The second most lethal person in the world is a spouse. The most lethal person in the world is an ex-spouse."

"Did you say there were four people involved in the fight?"

"Yeah. The guy with the spray, the guy who got sprayed, the Aussie and a fourth guy who the Aussie said attacked him. We haven't found that guy yet either."

"One· of the combatants in coach is from Australia? I'm expecting an Aussie friend on this train."

"Yes. There are lots of international passengers. This is The Canadian, the trans-Canada train from Vancouver. It runs two times a week in the summer."

"Where have you got the Aussie?"

"We're holding him for questioning."

"Sorry, excuse me a moment." I called Katya and asked her if she had spoken with Jack. He hadn't answered his phone, so I told her she could go home.

"Okay, how did you ID Hana?" I asked. "Have you got photo ID?"

"We found a Japanese passport with her picture in her purse. The name matches the booking for the cabin."

The second cop, Hunter, handed me a burgundy-coloured passport. Surprisingly, the name Hana Sato was written in upper case English on the information page. While the others stood back, I swung open the compartment door and walked in.

There was an L-shaped leather couch that probably transformed into a bed at night. A thin Asian woman, dressed in a pink sheath dress, was in a semi-recumbent position on the couch, her feet on the floor, her head on the cushion. I held the passport picture beside her face. At best, they were similar. Given the circumstances, I knew that she was the same Hana I had met on the Rocky Mountaineer.

I lifted her eyelids and saw that her pupils were pinpoint. That might go with narcotic poisoning, which causes constricted pupils. She was still warm, with no rigor mortis or lividity. She had vomited and also soiled her undergarments. There were no needle marks on her arms, drug paraphernalia or signs of head trauma. She might have ruptured a cerebral aneurysm, but that generally caused fixed, dilated pupils.

There was a small suitcase on the end of the bench seat. I flipped the lid up and found clothing, neatly sorted and packed into zippered, mesh-fabric cubes. A door in the compartment opened into a private washroom containing a narrow vanity, sink and toilet. The décor was stainless steel. There were his and hers unzipped toiletry bags and two toothbrushes on a ledge. My living reflection loomed in the full-length mirror on the back of the door.

I attached the toe tag with Hana's name, date of birth and time of death to the slender ankle that had danced its last tango. Glancing through the curtainless cabin window, I could see people milling about on the platform. I opened the door to the hall, pulled my gloves off from the cuffs and tossed them into a corner before exiting.

Branko was waiting outside. "So, what do you think?"

"I don't know. I'm going to call the hospital to find out what's going on with her husband. They probably have the same thing. She'll need an autopsy, but don't call for body transport yet."

"Okay. Which funeral home do you want to use—Schade's or Christobel's."

"I don't care, but don't call them quite yet."

I walked a little way down the train corridor and dialled the number of the Coventry Hospital emergency department. After identifying myself, I asked to speak with the emergency physician on duty. Alexander Hinkle, whom I knew personally, picked up.

I asked, "Did you just get a guy from the Coventry train station?"

"Yeah. Hi Matt. He's in Resuss One."

"What do you think is going on with him? His wife is dead on a train. I'm at the train station with her."

"Big man, 70 years old. He came in unconscious, with wheezing and shortness of breath. He might have asthma or heart failure. I wonder if he's had a brainstem stroke because his pupils are constricted and his heart rate is very slow. I gave him naloxone in case it's narcotics, but it had no effect. I've just gotten him intubated. He's going for a CT of his head in a few minutes."

"I don't think it's a stroke," I said. "His wife's pupils are just the same. It would be fantastically unlikely that they both had brainstem strokes on the same day—unless they're identical twins, which they're not, obviously. I think it's toxicologic. How much atropine have you given?"

"I've given him three doses of 0.6 milligrams. His heart rate is still in the low forties."

"If it's organophosphorus poisoning, you can give a lot more."

"How much can I give?"

"Just keep giving it until you get to 5 milligrams. That's eight ampoules of 0.6 milligrams."

"That's a lot."

"I know," I said.

After a brief pause and the clacking of computer keys, Alexander said, "I just googled organophosphorus poisoning. Keep giving atropine until you see the heart rate pick up. Go as high as 10 mg or 16 amps. They also recommend pralidoxime."

"Is he weak? Yes, give it."

"Like I said, I had to intubate him and put him on a ventilator. He was struggling to breathe with tons of secretions. That fits with what you said."

"Good man. Have you got pralidoxime? That might reverse some of the weakness."

"I'll call the hospital pharmacy."

"You may have to have it couriered from Toronto."

"Okay thanks. Gotta go."

"Okay wait. What's his name?"

"John Hartley."

"Does he have a beefy, red face and a white beard?"

"Yes," Alexander said impatiently.

"Had he shit his pants?"

"Yes. I heard he had food poisoning."

"I don't think so. That shouldn't kill you or at least not right away. Incontinence also goes with organophosphorus poisoning. Okay bye. Thanks Alex."

"Bye."

Returning to where Branko was standing, I said, "I think they either both overdosed or were both poisoned. I'm going to call my Regional Supervising Coroner about how long I can hold up the train."

"Poisoning might fit with a love-triangle jealousy motive. Did I overhear you say something about organophosphorus? That's insecticide, isn't it?"

"Yes. Insecticide and also nerve gas, like sarin and VX."

Branko's eyebrows went up. "Like sarin that was used in the Tokyo subway attack?"

"Yes. Did you find any Japanese terrorists on the train?"

"Well, *she's* Japanese. I'll find out," Branko said. He pulled out his phone and made a call. "Let's get this whole area taped off. Get all the passengers into the waiting room and close the train station. Lock the door to the platform and put a man on the door to the street. Nobody leaves until they've been screened. Get the fire department out here with hazmat suits. And see if you can get a passenger list."

Branko rushed off down the corridor and out of the train leaving Hunter to guard the door to the compartment. I took out my phone to call Richard Tull, the Regional Supervising Coroner, and then put it back on my belt. Before speaking with him, I needed more information about the husband to have a better picture of what was going on.

59

Chapter 9

The doctors' parking lot at Coventry General Hospital was full, so I drove my SUV over the concrete sidewalk barrier into the pay, public lot. I rushed down the corridor to the emergency department and found Alexander at the nursing station.

"Hey Alex, how's John Hartley?"

"His head CT was normal. He's upstairs in the ICU."

"So, still alive."

"We actually do stock pralidoxime in the pharmacy, so I gave him a dose before he left. They keep it because of all the farmers around here who use pesticide. Apparently, one of them ingested pesticide a few years ago when his wife left him. I don't think it made any difference toward getting his wife back."

"Because he was dead?"

"Yes."

"How much atropine did you end up giving?"

"He had 5 amps, so 3 milligrams. His heart rate was still in the forties when he left."

"Okay thanks. I'll go up and see him. Oh, one more thing. Where are his clothes?"

"We cut them off. They're in a plastic bag."

"Send anyone who handled his clothes for a shower. Don't open the plastic bag again. Save it for me. I'll write you a Warrant to Seize for it."

"Why would I need that? Just take them. The clothes probably went up to the ICU with him under his stretcher." Alexander turned and said to the nurse, "I'm going for a shower. Could you check on the guy who was pepper sprayed in the face."

"What?" I asked. "Did he come from the train?"

"I don't know. I had to deal urgently with Hartley. I didn't get a chance to speak with him yet."

"What bay is he in?"

"He's at the eyewash station. I'm going to get ophthalmology to see him." Alexander walked briskly toward the staff change room.

"His eyelids are swollen shut. We had to lead him in by the hand," the nurse said.

The eyewash station consisted of two giant plastic bags of saline suspended over a sink. A man with a dark brush cut was holding plastic tubing, directing the flow of salt water through the eyes of another who was hunched over the sink. They looked like construction workers out for a round of golf, dressed in new-looking, baggy shorts and pastel shirts.

"Hi. I'm Dr. Matthew Kork. Could I ask you a few questions? What happened to your friend?" I didn't tell them I was a coroner and not an emergency physician.

"Some crazy guy walked up to him and sprayed him in the face."

The spraying victim's face was beet red and his eyelids were in spasm. "Try to open your friend's eyelids to get the water into his eyes. Were you on the train?"

"What train? We are on holiday to visit with our cousins."

"Did you know the person who did this?"

"We don't know this man and we don't want to know him. I didn't think you had such lunatics in Canada. We just wanted to see

61

the CN Tower and visit with our cousins." His tone invited commis-
eration.

"Where are you from?"

"Ukraine."

"Slava Ukraini," I said. This translated to, *Glory to Ukraine.*

"Heroyam slava," he answered. *Glory to the heroes* was the
standard response.

"Can you see anything?" I asked the victim.

"No," he said through the water streaming over his face.

I put up another large bag of saline to replace the one which was
nearly empty. "You'd better run another full bag through his eyes."

"Can I have some eyedrops for my friend, Doctor?"

"There is an ophthalmologist coming. We're going to get an eye
specialist to examine your friend."

Climbing the stairs to the fourth floor, two at a time, I arrived at
the ICU. The desk clerk told me Hartley was in room five. I thanked
her and found the room. Looking through the plate glass window, I
could see a large motionless body attached to a mechanical
ventilator. I dialled Branko's number.

"What's up, Matt?"

"I'm at Coventry General Hospital. I'm pretty sure the guy who
got bear sprayed on the train is in the emergency department. The
nurses have his friend flushing his very inflamed eyes with saline.
They say they're Ukrainian tourists and don't know anything about
trains."

"I'd like to speak with them," Branko said. "Keep them there."

"They're waiting to see an ophthalmologist. I'm in the ICU with
Hartley."

"Has he woken up?"

"No. I'm just going in to check on him."

"Okay, thanks." Branko said and hung up.

After donning disposable gloves and a mask, I entered room five. The man I knew from the Rocky Mountaineer was lying in bed, attached to several intravenous infusions. There was an endotracheal tube protruding from his mouth, connected to a ventilator circuit. The EKG monitor showed that his heart rate was in the high thirties.

I listened to his chest and lifted his eyelids to confirm that his pupils were constricted. Everything else that I needed to know was displayed on the monitors. George Stefaniuk, the internist on call, was waiting outside the room to speak with me when I came out.

"How's he doing?" I asked.

"Hanging in. I heard you think he's been poisoned."

"It crossed my mind. His wife is dead on a train. They both have pinpoint pupils and incontinence. He's unconscious and bradycardic. His lungs are wet and wheezy. It all fits with an organophosphorus compound—you know, insecticide."

"I called the Ontario Poison Centre in Toronto and printed off their sheet for organophosphate poisoning—atropine, pralidoxime, diazepam, respiratory support. Questionable benefit from pralidoxime. I've got an atropine infusion running now."

"His heart rate is still low."

"I told the nurse to put the transthoracic pacemaker pads on his chest in case we need them. I don't think she's done it yet. The differential diagnosis includes organophosphorus insecticides, Sarin, VX nerve agent, Novichok and neostigmine from an anesthesiologist's toolkit. You didn't do it, did you?"

"No. Where are his clothes, George?"

"I don't know." He peered through the window into the room. "There's a big cinched plastic bag on the floor in the corner."

I looked through the window again and saw the bag. "I need to seize the clothes for a coroner's investigation. Can you make sure that no one touches them and send anyone who touched the bag for a shower?"

"Okay… Novichok is like something out of a spy movie. It's what the Russians used in Britain to poison some defectors. Spray on their front doorknob, wasn't it?"

"Yes," I said. "Sergei Skripal was a Russian double agent who was traded to the West in a spy swap. His daughter Yulia was visiting him in England. Can you order a Novichok level?"

"I doubt it."

"Can you order a cholinesterase level? Organophosphorus insecticides and the rest of the drugs you mentioned are cholinesterase inhibitors. That's how they work."

"It won't identify the agent, but okay."

"What about an isoproterenol infusion to speed up his heart?"

"That's two good ideas. I'm also thinking of inserting a temporary transvenous pacemaker in case his heart rate falls any farther," George said. "I'll have to put in a central venous line for the pacing wire and pressor drugs, unless you want to do it." Internists had extensive, primarily theoretical knowledge. Their training didn't emphasize practical skills.

"I can't. I have to go back to the train station," I said. "I don't think his blood is especially dangerous, unless it's Novichok."

"You're not really serious about that, are you?"

"I don't know. Both of the Skripals survived, so you should be okay to do the central line. Gown, mask, gloves, goggles should be enough protection," I encouraged him. "I don't think you have PAPR, do you?"

This was a hood with powered air filtration. I was very glad that I had only touched the doorhandle to Hartley's compartment on the train with gloved hands. My phone was buzzing on my hip. "Sorry, I have to take this."

Richard Tull, my supervisor, was on the line. "What the fuck is going on, Matthew? Did you seize a train at Coventry Station?"

"I was just about to call you," I said. "I wanted to speak with you about whether I was allowed to, and if so, what the procedure was and for how long."

"You prepare an Authority to Seize, sign it and hand it to the station master. You better tell me what's going on first."

There was silence after I told Richard what I knew. He was thinking. "What about botulism? Have you called Public Health?"

"Botulism causes paralysis, not loss of consciousness. And I think it's more gradual in onset. Her husband's unconscious. No one else on the train was sick."

"If it's lethal, then it does cause loss of consciousness, Matt. Maybe we should alert the Provincial Emergency Operations Centre in Toronto. They can get more hazmat suits out there. Don't take any scene photos. If this is a homicide, you'll have evidence on your phone and get dragged into court. Just tell the police what you want pictures of. That way only the forensic pathologist has to go."

"Okay."

"Call Public Health to check the food on the train. Go back to the train station. I'll call you back."

I googled the number for Somerset County Public Health. I got an answering machine with instructions to leave a message, voiced by someone who sounded like they were 16-years-old. I googled botulism next. It caused fixed, dilated pupils, not pinpoint pupils.

Detouring through the emergency department on my way back to my car, I went to the eyewash station. There was no one there, so I went to the nursing station to ask about the Ukrainians. A uniformed cop was leaning casually on the counter, chatting up a nurse.

"Where is the guy with pepper spray in his eyes?" I asked.

The nurse said, "They're both gone. I went to check on them, but they weren't in the department any longer."

65

"Did you see which way they went or what they were driving?" the cop asked.

"Sorry. They didn't go past the desk. We're run off our feet, so maybe we just didn't notice them."

"What ID did they give you?" I asked.

She handed me a page of printed identification stickers. One sticker was meant to be affixed to the top of each page in a patient's chart. They were blank except for the name, Roman Melnyk.

She said, "We rushed him through without any paperwork because it was an emergency. His friend was supposed to come back to reception to finish the registration."

"I'll call the cab companies and car rental places to check if anyone saw them," the cop said.

After washing my hands again really thoroughly, I walked past the dozen patients in cubicles waiting for attention, avoiding their stares. I strode through the full emergency department waiting room, thanking heaven that I wasn't an emergency physician anymore. I found my car and drove back over the concrete sidewalk barrier into the doctors' lot so I wouldn't have to pay for parking when I exited onto the street.

Chapter 10

The sun was high in the sky and there was a light breeze coming through the window of my vehicle. For some people, it was a perfect summer's day. They would go to Bayfield Beach on Lake Huron, spread their blanket out on the sand, frolic in the waves, have lunch in a trendy restaurant, browse the shops. For others, not so much.

Turning onto Railway Drive, I could see a group of people standing on the sidewalk outside the station. There were no parking spaces left in the lot. I parked behind a police car, tossed the plasticized coroner banner from my coroner bag onto the dashboard and exited with my bag slung over my shoulder. Approaching the crowd, I recognized the newlywed airline pilot and his wife from lunch on the Rocky Mountaineer.

"Bonjour Laurent and Celeste. Do you remember me?" I asked.

"Yes. We had lunch. Were you on this train too, Matthieu? We didn't see you," Celeste replied in lightly accented English.

"I live here in Coventry. I don't know whether I told you that I'm a coroner. I help police with death investigations."

"So. She was dead," Laurent said.

"Do you know who I am talking about?"

"Yes. The police already spoke with us. They took our statements. We're waiting to find out when we can get back on the train."

I didn't tell them that to some degree that depended on me. "I know you already told police, but please tell me again what you saw happen on the train." I pulled the coroner badge out of my bag to show them. I wasn't accustomed to doing this because Coventry was a small community and so far, there had been no coroner-imposters.

"Our compartment was across the hall from the Asian lady and her husband," Laurent said. "We were the ones to find her."

"Had she been ill?"

"Yes, we could hear her vomiting," Celeste said. "Could Covid kill you so instantly, Matthieu?"

"No, it's not likely."

"We had an early breakfast," Laurent continued. "After our neighbours came back from the restaurant, I went to tell them that there was a man in their compartment while they were gone. I thought he might be making up the bed, but he wasn't wearing a uniform. I went across to have a look in case he was a thief. Only the concierge and other passengers were allowed in our rail car."

"What was he doing?"

"Nothing that I saw. He was just coming out of their washroom. He said he was staying in another compartment but had to use the toilet as an emergency because he was feeling sick."

"Did you see him going through their luggage?"

"No, but I was still suspicious that he was looking for something to steal. Their suitcase was unzipped on the seat. I asked them whether they had left it like that."

"What did they say?"

"The man looked angry. He wanted to know what the guy looked like. He looked through his suitcase. Then he went back out, maybe to look for the guy. We could hear her vomiting after he left, so Celeste went across to see if she could help."

"Yes, that was when she looked very sick," Celeste said. "I went to tell Laurent to get help. When he came back with the conductor, we could see that she wasn't moving. The conductor locked the door to the compartment. When we arrived in Coventry, there were police and an ambulance waiting outside."

"How far were you from Coventry when you found her?"

"About 20 minutes, I think," Celeste said.

"Did you give a description of the man who was in their compartment to police?"

"Yes. He was about 40 or 50 years old, five feet ten inches tall, dark hair, brush cut, muscular." Laurent said.

"What was he wearing? Had you seen him before on the train?"

"I never saw him before. He was wearing short pants and a tennis shirt. He wouldn't look at me."

"Please don't let this ruin your honeymoon, Celeste and Laurent. The train will be delayed here for a few hours while police gather evidence." Then, as an awkward afterthought, I said, "Bonnes fêtes!" which means happy holidays. It didn't really fit the occasion.

There was now yellow police tape, tarps and tents up around the section of the train that I had been in earlier. There were also a lot more cops. Branko was standing on the platform talking to Hunter. He came over to usher me through.

"Who are all these guys, Branko?" I asked.

"The VIA Rail Police and the Ontario Provincial Police are here, and we called some of our own officers in early before their shifts to help interview passengers. No obvious terrorists so far."

"Did you find the two Ukrainian guys from the hospital ER?"

"We checked with both cab companies. Nobody fitting their description took a cab from the hospital in the last hour. We're checking the car rental agencies."

"Okay. I'll phone the forensic pathologist on call to tell him I'm sending her for an autopsy. I'm not sure how we're going to arrange body transport. The funeral homes will be reluctant. They wear business suits, not hazmat suits."

"The OPP is sending their UCRT team. They might look after it."

"What's UCRT stand for?"

"It's the Urban Search and Rescue Team."

"Isn't search spelled with an *S*?"

"It is, isn't it. The *C* might stand for chemicals. They're specialists in gathering evidence from dangerous or contaminated scenes. Also, counter-terrorism, which starts with *C*."

"I'm going to be embarrassed if it's not Novichok," I said. "Where's the Aussie you were telling me about?"

"He's sitting in the back seat of one of the cruisers." Branko checked his notebook. "His name is Jack Rielly. Rielly said that Hartley staggered into the passenger car where he was sitting and asked to see the can of bear spray, which he knew Jack carried in his pack. Hartley took this can and sprayed another passenger in the face. A third passenger got up and shocked Hartley with a Taser.

Rielly got up because it was his bear spray. He asked the Taser guy if he was a cop, and the guy tried to tase him too, so then they started whaling on each other. This was just before the train pulled into Coventry station."

"Shit. I know Jack. That was my bear spray."

"Your bear spray? How is that possible?"

"He was carrying it back from Banff for me. It's not allowed on airplanes."

"What do you know about Jack Rielly?"

"Not much. I met him on holiday in Jasper. He lost his son in a motorcycle accident, and then his wife left him. He came to Canada to forget."

"Tough break."

"He's supposed to be staying with me for a couple of days."

"Well, I don't think we'll be laying charges. It depends on what the Ukrainians have to say."

"Okay. I'll call the pathologist in Toronto to alert him that she's coming."

It was Ron Rasmussen who picked up. "Hi Ron. It's Matthew Kork. I'm an Investigating Coroner in Coventry. We've worked together before."

"Yes, I know you, Matthew. What's up?"

"I'm sending you the body of Hana Sato from a train that's parked here. She's a 48-year-old passenger who died on board this morning just before it pulled into Coventry. Her husband was taken off the train, deathly ill. He's in Coventry General Hospital, unconscious on a ventilator. They both got sick soon after having breakfast on board—vomiting and diarrhea. They both have pinpoint pupils. The husband's heart rate is in the thirties."

"The state of dilation of pupils is an unreliable post-mortem sign. If they're constricted, you probably saw her quite soon after death. If you check her in an hour, they'll be different, probably mid-dilation."

"Her husband's pupils are pinpoint as well. I don't think it's narcotics. Naloxone didn't have any effect on the husband."

"Fentanyl is commonly laced with xylazine to extend the high. Naloxone won't reverse xylazine. The likeliest cause is narcotic and xylazine intoxication."

"That doesn't explain their gastrointestinal symptoms. Also, the husband was wheezing and struggling to breathe in emerge."

"What are you thinking, Matt? It doesn't sound like food poisoning. She died too quickly. You said it was right after breakfast?"

"I'm thinking poisoning with an organophosphorus chemical. Possibly a suicide pact. Can you test for things like Sarin, VX or Novichok?"

"That's a little far-fetched. No, we can't. I think that a military-affiliated lab in the States could. She wouldn't have had access to any

71

of those chemicals anyway. If it's an organophosphorus compound, it's probably insecticide. An insecticide would have a foul taste, so they wouldn't have taken it by accident."

"There's more to the story. The husband went on a rampage attacking another passenger on the train before collapsing."

"Could he have taken a hallucinogen?"

"He attacked the other passenger with bear spray. He seemed to be acting purposefully."

"Did you call Public Health to check the food on the train?" Ron asked.

"I'm still waiting for them to call back."

"Any other passengers with GI symptoms?"

"No."

"No suicide note?"

"No. Could you do a cholinesterase level? Organophosphorus compounds are cholinesterase inhibitors." I looked up to see two unmarked vans pulling into the train station parking lot. Six fit-looking guys wearing dark clothing climbed out.

"We may be able to do that. The routine toxicology screen includes narcotics and hallucinogens. I'm not going to ask for any of those other things. Do the police think it's criminally suspicious?"

"Possibly."

"Well, I'll speak with the police officers attending the autopsy tomorrow. If they think there's criminality, the lab can pivot to a full tox."

"Okay thanks. I think the OPP UCRT team has just arrived."

"What have you set in motion, Matthew?"

"Maybe they weren't doing anything and needed an outing."

I watched the team members unload several duffel bags and cases from their vans and pile the gear onto the train station platform. Air tanks and hazmat suits appeared from the duffel bags.

I got out my phone to text Jack. *How's she going, mate?*

After a minute, I got back, *All right thanks Matt. Made a little detour to the police station.*

Are you in trouble?

I'll let you know.

Do you need a lawyer?

An honest man shouldn't need one.

I'm not so sure.

I'm in a corner room by myself waiting for someone to question me.

If you're not out in two hours, I'll find a lawyer for you.

Thanks. Someone just came in.

I watched the activity on the platform and then went over and stood beside the officer who seemed to be in charge of the new arrivals. "So, what does URCT stand for?" I asked.

"And you are?"

"Dr. Matthew Kork, Investigating Coroner. I showed my badge for the second time that day."

"Oh, okay. I never remember. Here is what I think it is. UCRT is an acronym combining USAR and CBRNE. USAR is Urban Search and Rescue. CBRNE is Chemical, Biological, Radiological and Nuclear. RT is Response Team. Is she still inside?"

"As far as I know."

"We'll finish getting suited up and have a look. We were told possible organophosphate nerve gas poisoning."

"It may have been ingested," I said. "Both she and her husband were sick after having breakfast on the train. No other passengers were affected."

"Okay. We'll bag all of her clothing and personal effects anyway."

"The Centre of Forensic Sciences in Toronto will only test biological specimens."

73

"That's okay. We'll take her stuff to decontaminate the train and keep it for future reference. We can make a request to Health Canada to test it."

"She's going for an autopsy. Can you also put her in a bag? The funeral home transport guys will be dressed in ties and jackets. When can we call them?"

"We'll need a couple of hours."

Two burly men in grey police uniforms with a leashed German shepherd came over and stood beside us.

"What's the dog for?" I asked.

"He's our bomb sniffer," one of them answered.

"Dr. Kork, these are the VIA Rail Police," the OPP UCRT officer said.

"Hi, I'm Matthew Kork, the investigating coroner," I said.

"I'm Fogarty. This is Cleto." Fogarty held out his hand, which I fist bumped. "Would you like to see the front of train video, Doctor?"

"I don't think so. Do you have security cameras on board?"

"The newest trains do," he answered. "The station and platform are covered."

The dog was sitting, staring straight ahead indifferently. I looked it over without meeting its stare because you aren't supposed to look strange dogs in the eye.

"Don't pet the dog. He's working," Fogarty said.

"I don't pet German shepherds."

"Are you coming back on the train, Doctor?" the UCRT officer interrupted.

"I've seen her already. Well, there is one more thing I would like to check."

"Okay, suit up. You can't go back in there without a hazmat suit."

He handed me a disposable plastic suit, which I put on and zipped up. One of his team members fed my arms through the harness for the air tank. Breathing from our tanks, we boarded and traipsed down the hall to Hana Sato's compartment. I lifted her eye-lids and her pupils were now in mid-dilation. Exiting the train, I left my suit and nitrile gloves in a bin near the doorway.

The Medical Officer of Health for Somerset County called my cell as I was getting in my car to leave. She said that she would send a team of nurses to gather up any suspicious food stuffs in the train kitchen and send them for analysis. She also wanted fecal samples from John Hartley. I gave her George Stefaniuk's contact information at the hospital.

She concluded by saying, "It doesn't sound like botulism, but sometimes, we have to damn the expense and just go ahead and give botulism anti-toxin because laboratory confirmation can take several days."

"Speak to George Stefaniuk." I didn't need to share responsibility for this decision. It wasn't botulism anyway.

Two white vans with parabolic dishes on the roofs and the insignia of Global and CTV, both Canadian national news broadcasters, cruised past and reversed into illegal parking spots in front of me. They were as expert as blow flies in detecting the faintest odours of death from a tremendous distance. It was time for me to leave.

Chapter 11

The door bell rang, followed by a barrage of barking from Madame Fifi, our Bichon Frise. Summer, a thin 10-year-old girl who lived on our street, was standing on the front porch. Madame Fifi ran out, greeted Summer dutifully with a few licks, and then disappeared back into the house.

During Covid, when schools were closed, Summer patrolled our street, putting notes into people's mailboxes with hopeful messages like, *Stay strong!* and, *Have a nice day!*

"Can I walk Madame Fifi?" Summer asked. She did this free of charge for her own pleasure. Her parents wouldn't allow a dog.

"Yes, certainly. I'll get her leash."

"Have you been away?"

"Yes. We were out west for a train trip through the Rocky Mountains."

She looked at me closely. "Are you having a good day?"

I reflected on the events at the train station. "Just okay, Summer. How's your day going?"

"Well, if you're not having a good day—then—have a good day!"

"Thanks Summer." I went to search for the dog, who I knew would be hiding under the farthest reaches of the dining room table. She liked Summer, but Madame Fifi had reached middle-aged

76

complacency. Once I had dragged her out from under the table, put her passively resisting limbs through her harness and attached her leash, she and Summer pranced down the sidewalk together and out of sight.

Katya was in the kitchen working on a Sudoku puzzle in the newspaper. "Was that Summer at the door?"

"Yes. She says have a good day."

"What's going on at the train station?"

"It's unclear. One dead, one in hospital. I've released some sort of genie. Every police force in the country is converging on the train station."

"And that's your doing?"

"Yes, I think so."

"Do you remember my cousin Jadwiga?" Katya asked. "You met her in Poland. Curly hair. My mother and her grandmother were sisters."

"She was just a kid when I met her. She's a pediatrician now, right?"

"Yes. She just texted me that she's working as a live-in nanny in Wisconsin."

"That's strange. She must have taken a large cut in pay."

"Well, she's young and unattached and wants to see the world. I don't think Polish doctors get paid that well."

"She could be a doctor anywhere in the EU now. I can't imagine that there is anything much to see or do in Wisconsin."

"She'd never been to North America. She said that the little girl she's looking after has cancer and they needed somebody with medical qualifications to live in. Maybe they're paying her well. Anyway, she wants to come visit."

"She's welcome, I guess. When were you thinking?"

"We haven't sorted that out yet. Not for a couple of weeks. She has to ask for the time off."

"It seems like a lot of people are visiting their cousins in Coventry this summer. What are you going to do with her? Niagara Falls, I suppose."

"Oh, we'll just visit with my sister and her daughters and go out for a few meals and things. Family is important."

"Do you want me to take time off work?"

"No. It's okay. You can just join us on weekends."

"Weekends? How long is she staying?"

"If she stays a week, there would be a weekend on either side."

"Jack will be using our guest bedroom. I'm not sure how long he's staying."

"That's not a problem. It's just in the planning stage. Jadwiga hasn't even bought a ticket yet."

My phone rang on my belt and I swiped right to answer. "Hello, is this Dr. Kork?" There was an edge in the voice.

"Yes. Who is this?"

"My name is Micheline Labreque. I'm a Vice President of Customer Protective Services at VIA Rail in Montreal. The company's goal is to get an incident train rolling within 45 minutes. Studies have shown that passengers become unruly at 30 minutes, and that mob mentality takes over at 60 minutes. They begin breaking windows and forcing doors open. These deadlines have come and gone."

"The passengers have been unloaded and are being individually interviewed by police," I said.

"Be that as it may, the train itself is not part of the scene if the incident is non-chemical. It is also not evidence in any investigation. Our top priority is to get our rolling stock rolling. It should be yours as well. Can you give me an estimate of time as to when you'll release the train?"

"It might be chemical. I believe hours, not days. The train might have to be decontaminated. Can you disconnect the car where the incident occurred and move the rest?"

"You would be good with that? I'll look into it and get back to you. Will you be at this number?"

"Yes."

She hung up and I turned my attention back to Katya. "I was planning to make cedar-plank salmon on the barbeque tonight. I can't imagine that the police would hold Jack Rielly past dinner time."

"Who was that on the phone, hon?"

"VIA Rail. I'm going to be in trouble if I don't release their train."

"Can they do anything to you?"

"They can call my boss."

"The salmon sounds good, hon. I saw the cedar plank soaking in the kitchen sink beside a full bottle of Diana sauce. That's your go-to meal when you have special guests."

I chopped up red onions and green peppers and dumped them into a mixing bowl with half a bottle of Diana sauce. After laying the salmon out on the wet plank, I covered it with the topping. Jack called me late that afternoon from the police station to ask whether the offer of a visit was still on. The police told him he was free to go but not to leave Coventry. He was waiting with his suitcase on the curb outside the station when I pulled up.

I lowered the car window. "Hello Jack. Welcome to the wild west."

"Guddeye mate. Good to see you again." He looked thinner than I remembered and the lines on his face were more pronounced.

I opened the back hatch of my SUV to load his luggage. "Hop in Jack. I would show you a bit of the town, but dinner is waiting. When did you eat last?"

"Not since breakfast. The cops gave me a cup of coffee."

"Did they play good cop/bad cop, or did they go straight to the water boarding?"

"They wanted to know what I knew about John Hartley, and how it was that I supplied him with bear spray. Their ears perked up when I told them I got it from you."

"It's definitely a strange saga. I heard some of it from Detective Marcovic. Did you know John Hartley?"

"Marcovic was the name of the detective who interviewed me. He said he would probably have more questions for me once he located the other two guys from the train."

"Well, we're almost home. You can tell me the whole story over dinner."

I took the most scenic route following the street that paralleled the canal that bisected Coventry. Ducks and geese who lived on its banks were straddling the road and couldn't be bothered to get out of the way. Not wishing to leave a bad impression by nudging them along with my bumper, I waited for the road to clear.

"Canada geese love Coventry," I said. "The city runs herding dogs along the waterfront paths in the early morning when no one is watching, to convince them to leave. Their natural predators are coyotes, but that solution is worse than having to step over goose poop."

"It's a pretty town," Jack said politely.

Katya emerged from the front door as my vehicle pulled into the driveway. She took Jack by the arm that wasn't holding luggage and pulled him toward the house. "You've had quite the adventure and we're dying to hear all about it."

"Talk amongst yourselves while I pop the salmon on the barbie," I said.

"And there are some coconut shrimp appetizers in the oven."

"That sounds good, Katya."

We sat in the living room around a table of appetizers renewing old acquaintance. "So, how was the cross-country train trip?" Katya asked.

Jack didn't answer right away. Barbeque smoke was starting to waft from the back yard.

"Not counting the events of today," I said.

"It was good," he said cautiously. "The sleeper compartments were all sold out when I bought my ticket in Edmonton. I had a seat in economy. The seat reclined with a footrest like a La-Z-Boy chair at night."

"Were you able to shower?" Katya asked.

"No shower for three days."

"Well, you can shower here. Would you like to have one before dinner?"

"Maybe later tonight thanks, Katya. I washed my hair in the bathroom sink at the end of the rail car this morning."

"Make yourself entirely at home," Katya said. "Help yourself to anything in the fridge while you're here."

"Madame Fifi will wash your feet for you," I said. "Take your shoes off and sit back." The dog snapped to attention at the sound of her name, but Jack left his shoes on.

"Did you get the domed-glass-ceiling experience in the observation car?" Katya asked.

"Yeh. I went up there for a stretch. They had drinks and snacks."

"I've never seen the prairies," Katya said. "I hear they're flat. What did you think?"

"I could have given them a miss. It looks almost like Australia. I liked northern Ontario a lot."

"Is that where you met John Hartley and Hana Sato?" I asked.

"I was sitting in the observation car, the Skyline Car they call it, reading the label on the can of bear spray. We got to talking and John offered to buy it off me. I told him it wasn't mine to sell."

"Did he say why he wanted the spray? There's not much camping in Toronto."

"No. He said he was meaning to buy some and it would save him a trip. The label states it's concentrated capsaicin, pepper spray, with a range of 35 feet. Turns out he wanted a weapon."

"Did you visit his compartment?" I asked.

"Yes, once. I wanted to see what I was missing sitting in economy. I got to know John and his wife a bit over the three days. I told him I was visiting you, and it turned out he *knew* you. He knew all about you, what you do for a living and where you live in Coventry. I told him I was carrying the bear spray for you. That's a real coincidence."

"Did you know the guy he attacked."

"I'd never seen him before. Did you know him?"

"No. What about his friend?"

"Never seen him before either."

I could see through the window that smoke was now billowing out of the barbeque. "How long has the salmon been cooking?" I asked Katya.

"Twenty minutes."

"I better have a look." I went across the yard and lifted the barbeque lid. The bottom of the plank was on fire and the peppers and onions on the fish were starting to show some charring. Using two spatulas, I lifted the plank off the flames and onto a metal serving tray. My phone was ringing. It was a call that I was obligated to answer.

Richard Tull wanted an update on the situation at the train station. I told him that UCRT was on site and that I had spoken with the Medical Officer of Health and a representative from VIA Rail. She was eager to get the train moving, but I thought that the train should be decontaminated. He sighed and asked how sure I was about organophosphorus poisoning being the cause of death.

"I'm not sure at all, but it would explain all of the facts," I said.

"What about food borne botulism? Have you excluded it?"

"I believe botulism causes paralysis and dilated pupils but no loss of consciousness."

"If the poisoning victim dies, then that would result in loss of consciousness and fixed dilated pupils." He wasn't wrong, but John Hartley had constricted pupils.

"The Medical Officer of Health is going to discuss whether to give botulism anti-toxin on spec with the internist who is looking after the spouse."

Richard thanked me and said that he would make some calls.

Carrying the salmon on the still smoking plank on a metal tray into the house, I made a triumphant entry, laying it on trivets on the dining room table.

"That smells great!" Jack said.

I carved off three portions from the fish. It was a bit red in the middle, but it wouldn't transmit botulism.

"It's done perfectly!" Katya enthused.

"Good on ya, mate!" Jack said.

"Thanks. The secret is smoke and caramelized sugar. What were you saying about the two guys on the train, Jack?"

"I think they both got on after we reached Ontario. John came into the passenger car this morning and asked to see the spray can. He said it was to know what kind to buy. He was wheezing and smelled like shit. When I gave it to him, he walked down the aisle and just sprayed some poor bugger point-blank in the face. Then a third guy who was sitting behind me ran up and tasered John in the neck. John fell on the floor and didn't get up."

"The police told me you got into a fight with the third man."

"Not me, mate. I gave him a shove to get past him so I could help John. He said he was a cop, but I knew he wasn't."

"Why not?"

"Because he already knew the joker who got sprayed. He asked him, 'Are you all right, sir?' but then he was talking to him quietly after that and trying to get him up and moving toward the door. We were just pulling into the station. John was lying on the floor, not moving, and they just stepped over him. I stood in their way to stop them from getting off. He had the gun in his free hand and tried to shock me, so I chopped down on his arm and he dropped it."

"Did he try to pick it up?"

"No. He tried to chop me in the neck, but he was off balance with the train moving and holding his friend up, and hit me in the chest."

"You were chopping each other?"

"I have a black belt in karate."

"Really. Was John conscious?"

"Yes."

"Did he say anything?"

"He said to check on his wife. I didn't get a chance to go because everyone was shouting and dialling 911. They weren't speaking English. The two guys were talking in some Slavic language. 'Harasho' and 'Davai.' "

"I might have met them in the Coventry Hospital emergency department. They were both about 40-years-old, five foot ten, brush cuts, muscular."

"Yeh. They looked like rugby players. Baggy shorts and polo shirts."

"How did the police react to your story?"

"The detective, Marcovic, took notes and recorded the interview. He asked me the same questions as you a few different ways."

"I believe you, Jack," Katya said.

"Thanks a heap."

"Did the guy you judo chopped have a mole on his left cheek?" I asked.

"Yeh, I think so."

"Okay. Have some more salmon, Jack. What do you think of doing Niagara Falls tomorrow?" I asked.

"I don't think I'm allowed to leave Coventry."

"Well, thanks anyway for carrying the bear spray back. Is there any left for me to use?"

"No worries, mate." His tone was less than enthusiastic. "The cops are holding onto it for you now. Was it just a coincidence that you gave it to me to carry?"

"Yes. I'm not part of an international conspiracy."

A few moments of uncomfortable silence followed. I don't know that he believed me.

Chapter 12

Niagara Falls, Ontario

In the morning, I found Jack fully dressed and sitting in the kitchen, looking out of the window listlessly. He might have been wishing that he had never met me. Katya had told him to make full use of the kitchen facilities, but it didn't look like he had eaten anything.

I made him some toast and a cup of upmarket coffee with my espresso machine. Since he couldn't leave, I asked whether he would be interested in seeing the sights of Coventry. He agreed without much ardor. We were interrupted by Richard Tull calling me on my cell. I excused myself and went to my study to answer it.

Richard said that the entire train had been shifted to a side track where it was still parked. The UCRT team had finished their work. An emergency toxic spills cleanup team had scrubbed down Hana Sato's compartment. The funding had to be approved by his supervisor, the Deputy Chief Coroner. He was getting extreme pressure to get the train moving.

A VIA Rail vice president had just called him. The company's goal was to get an incident train rolling within 45 minutes. The company had had to charter buses to transport passengers late in the evening the rest of the way to Toronto. The train had been out of service for a day. They had a new crew ready and standing by in Coventry. Did I have any objection to his releasing the train?

I was afraid to think what all that might have cost. Of course, I didn't have any objection. I was grateful and a little surprised that Richard had been so supportive of my assessment. I had told them that they could move the train if they disconnected Hana Sato's car. My sincere hope was that my clinical judgement had been correct. I didn't tell Richard, but I was beginning to doubt whether it was.

I texted Branko to ask if Jack and I could go to Niagara Falls. He said to give him one more day to find the Ukrainians. If we went the next day, we shouldn't get any ideas about escaping across the border over the Rainbow Bridge. I said that the pot of gold at the end of the rainbow was on our side of the border.

My next call was to the intensive care unit to find out how John Hartley was doing. His nurse told me that he was still unconscious and on a ventilator. My vanity told me that I needed to see for myself whether he needed that because I had a skill set that internists and ICU staff didn't possess.

Re-entering the kitchen, I found Katya sitting with Jack, eating scrambled eggs. Katya was making uplifting chatty noises, asking him how he had slept and reinforcing that he should help himself to anything in the kitchen whenever he wanted. I took a seat at the table with them and said, "Would you mind very much if I made a quick detour to the hospital?"

"Do you really have to go?" Katya asked plaintively.

"That's fine, mate," Jack said.

"I won't be long. The guy from the train is still unconscious. I need to check on him."

"How about a walking tour then, Jack?" Katya asked. "We have shops, a waterfront, a small art gallery and a small museum like any other self-respecting small city."

"That sounds good. Don't go to a lot of trouble though, Katya."

After arriving at the hospital, I went to the surgical suite and borrowed a nerve stimulator from one of the operating rooms that wasn't in use. Through the window of his room in the ICU, I could see John's portly figure and his chest rising and falling in time with the ventilator bellows. I donned gown, cap, face shield and gloves and entered the room.

Except for his mechanical breathing, John lay motionless. His monitors showed a heart rate in the fifties. I attached two electrodes to the skin of his forearm over the ulnar nerve and clipped the nerve stimulator wires to them. There was no response to the electrical current. When I exited, his nurse told me that they were still suctioning copious secretions from his endotracheal tube.

As I was returning the nerve stimulator to the O.R., the head nurse ran over to me and asked me to please give the anesthetic for an emergency Caesarean section. They would otherwise have to pull an anesthesiologist out of an elective operating room and delay that room. Seeing us conferring, the obstetrician came over and said that she couldn't wait for any elective case to finish. The fetal heart rate monitor was non-reassuring and there was meconium, or fetal stool, in the amniotic fluid.

I was sorry that I had gone back to the O.R. With this sort of pressure, I couldn't refuse. If it truly was an emergency, I would have blood on my hands, and instant notoriety. I did the case and happily both the baby and the mother were fine. Although they stressed out obstetricians, the signs indicating fetal distress weren't that reliable.

Instead of tempting fate by going back to the O.R. one more time, I dropped the nerve stimulator outside John Hartley's room in the ICU. I told his nurse to call the O.R. head nurse to come and get it. On my way out, Ron Rasmussen called with the preliminary autopsy report on Hana Sato.

"Hi Matt. Can you talk?"

I took a seat at the nursing station and took out pen and paper to transcribe the result. "Yes, go ahead."

"Thanks to you, I had to do the autopsy wearing a hazmat suit. I hope it really was worth all the trouble. There was no apparent anatomic cause of death. Hana Sato's heart, lungs and brain looked grossly normal. I've reserved these organs for histological examination. Her lungs were heavy, probably due to pulmonary edema fluid. That goes with narcotic overdose."

"It could be negative pressure pulmonary edema, secondary to breathing against an obstructed upper airway."

"Pulmonary edema is a well recognized complication of narcotic overdose."

"The standard anesthetic for cardiac surgery is massive doses of narcotics. Narcotics never cause pulmonary edema in that situation because the anesthesiologist maintains an open airway with an endotracheal tube."

"Well, we've had this discussion before. It's in the literature. It's due to histamine release and capillary leak. We'll get confirmation when the toxicology comes back."

Ron was an excellent pathologist with a narrow field of view. I felt like I was the expert here with real world experience. Only morphine commonly released histamine. "Were you able to order organophosphate levels?"

"I ordered a full tox," he said. "That tests for hundreds of compounds, including all the newer designer narcotics. I checked the list and there are no insecticides on it. I'll request that manually in the comments. I'm releasing her body. There's a glut of bodies in the morgue right now. Is anyone coming to collect her remains?"

"You might have to hold onto them until we find out whether her husband is waking up. The police are still tracing family in Japan."

I found the cell number for the Director of the Forensic Sciences Laboratory in the contacts list on my phone. I only had it because he had put it on a slide at a conference that I had attended where expert speakers made a display of appearing magnanimous and accessible.

The Director informed me that full toxicology normally took 80 days. He could prioritize my case to one to two weeks if there was a threat to public safety, or detention of an accused depended on the result. Their lab didn't have methods for testing for organophosphates or even to do a pseudocholinesterase level. The decision to send blood to outside labs that could do this was at the discretion of the Chief Coroner of the province.

I asked that he please prioritize it and rang off. It would be improper for me to contact the Chief Coroner. Any communication with him would have to go up the chain of command. I would have to be satisfied with the pseudocholinesterase level that George Stefaniuk was doing on John Hartley. I couldn't have ordered it myself as a coroner. The coroners' service had no jurisdiction because he was still alive.

When I got back home, there was a tall slender young woman with straight shoulder-length blonde hair, about thirty years of age, standing with Katya in the driveway. She had high Slavic cheekbones and was wearing bright red lipstick. She wore a simple wrap dress and held herself in a pleasing way. They were speaking in Polish.

"Hi Matt. You remember Jadwiga," Katya said.

I was astonished to see her so soon. I suspected that Katya had not been telling me the whole truth about her visit. "Hi Jadwiga. Katya told me you might be coming."

"Yes, hello Matthias. I am very happy to be here," she answered in accented English.

"Your English is very good, Jadwiga."

"Oh, thank you so much. I have been studying it for many years. You have a very nice house. May I use your bathroom please?"

"Of course," Katya said. "I'll show you the way."

Katya looked at me and then moved her eyes to Jadwiga's suitcase indicating that I was meant to attend to it. Katya and Jadwiga disappeared into the house with me following, the wheels of the suitcase bumping over the cracks in the sidewalk.

I left the suitcase in the foyer and caught up to Katya in the kitchen. I whispered, "I thought you said she would be coming in a couple of weeks."

"I know. That's what I thought. She texted me from the bus station that she was here."

"She looks different."

"Fifteen years will do that."

"Jack's still here. Where are you going to put her?"

"We have a four-bedroom house. I'll just move some of the crap out of Michael's old bedroom for her."

"How long is she staying?"

"I don't know. She didn't say."

"You should find out. Does she have a ticket home?"

"I didn't want to embarrass her by asking her that when she's only just arrived," Katya whispered. "She would need a ticket back to Poland to get into the country, wouldn't she?"

"I don't know."

The toilet flushed and Jadwiga emerged from the bathroom with refreshed makeup. Madame Fifi was walking lockstep and must have been in the bathroom with her. When Jadwiga arrived in the kitchen, the dog sat staring up at her, fascinated.

"How was your trip, Jadwiga? Would you like a cup of tea?" I asked.

"Yes. It was very good thank you. I have had no problem in crossing the border. In my Polish passport I have a 90-days visa for the USA and Canada."

"Sit down. Make yourself at home, Jadwiga," I said, filling the tea kettle with fresh water. "We have another guest, Jack Rielly from Australia, staying with us. I hope you like him."

"I think I will like him very much." She and Katya exchanged glances.

"Katya told me you were looking after a little girl with cancer in Wisconsin."

"Yes. They do not have so many good places to look after her in Wisconsin. She was very sick. I was giving her chemotherapy in the home. Now she is dead."

"I'm so sorry, Jadwiga. Were you very close with her?"

"Yes. It is very sad. She was only eight years old."

"Are you going back for her funeral or for the rest of your belongings?"

"The rest of my belongings are here. I will visit with you now if it is okay."

"Of course, Jadwiga. Stay as long as you like. We'll show you around. Where do you think we should go, Katya—Elora, Stratford, Bayfield?"

"She wants to see Niagara Falls," Katya said, and Jadwiga nodded her approval almost imperceptibly.

"Where's Jack?" I asked.

"He said he needed some exercise. He borrowed your bike. You were gone a long time."

"Did you do a tour of the city?"

"No, not yet," Katya said. "I thought I would wait until Jadwiga arrived."

When Jack got home, we made the introductions. Jadwiga and Jack smiled and shook hands, but it seemed a little awkward. I was thinking the more the merrier, and that Jadwiga might provide Jack with a distraction. As he was free to travel the next day, we made plans to visit Niagara Falls.

My cousin's 10-year-old son Lembitu from Estonia had stayed with us a few years previously, and we had taken him to Niagara Falls. When he saw it from the sidewalk vantage point where most tourists congregate, his comment was, "I thought it would be higher." In fact, I thought it would be higher too. It had seemed higher in my memory.

I explained to him that it wasn't the highest, but it was the largest-by-volume cataract in the world. Twenty years ago, Katya and I had taken the Maid of the Mist boat that went to the bottom of the Falls, and it had seemed high enough on that day. During Lembitu's stay, we also attended a Toronto Bluejays baseball game, visited Canada's Wonderland and Bayfield Beach on Lake Huron. He said that they had very similar things in Estonia. People lie to uphold national pride.

We got up early and were on the road by 9 a.m. The drive to Niagara Falls takes about two and a half hours. Jack and I, having the longest legs, sat in front and Katya and Jadwiga sat in the back. It was hard to make conversation because of the noise my SUV made on the highway. We were mainly prodding Jadwiga and Jack to make comparisons between Australia and Poland with respect to the quality of medical care and motorcycles.

Determined not to make the same mistake twice, I didn't approach Niagara Falls head on. Instead, I drove well east of it, to the Niagara River gorge, which is downstream and grand in its own right. Following the Niagara Parkway, there are several scenic spots for cars to pull over. We took some group photos and our guests seemed suitably impressed.

Creeping closer to the cataract, we arrived at the loading station for the boats that took tourists upstream along the river. We were issued raincoats, boarded a vessel and congregated with other passengers at the bow. We could faintly hear but could not yet see

Niagara. As the boat drew closer, the noise became deafening, until we were surrounded by a panorama of cascading water.

I noticed Jadwiga edging closer to Jack and then clutching his arm, which he did not object to. The spray from the Falls hit our raincoats and drenched our hair. It was truly awe inspiring, and I felt that where once I had failed, today I had achieved my objective. I took a picture of our two guests with their hair plastered to their heads and water streaming down their faces. Jadwiga wiped away her running mascara with a tissue and she looked even prettier without it.

We weren't quite done with Niagara. The waxen version of the tallest man in the world astonished us at Ripley's Believe It or Not. Kindly butterflies alighted on Jadwiga's hair at the Butterfly Conservatory. There is something for everyone in the city of Niagara Falls. Before leaving, Katya asked Jack if he would like to sit in the back of the car with Jadwiga. It was too soon and he looked uncomfortable with the suggestion. I said that men should sit in front where they could manspread their legs.

Chapter 13

Despite a group text to my anesthesia colleagues, I wasn't able to get another week off from the operating room. I still had three working days. Katya, Jack and Jadwiga went out touring our region by bicycle together. We had enough as my son Michael still stored his bikes with us.

I had an anesthetic list in the urology room on Monday. In the morning, I went to the operating room to get a nerve stimulator and visited John Hartley in the ICU before starting. He was still sedated and on a ventilator. The sedation was to avoid possible distress from being awake and paralyzed.

This was his day five in the unit. The nurses and doctors had spoken to him during his semi-lucid periods but he was unconscious again now. I attached the nerve stimulator to his forearm. When I activated it, there was a flicker of a twitch. He was making progress but was far from being able to breathe on his own.

Back in the operating room, the first of a series of bladder tumour patients was brought in. They were all elderly current or ex-smokers. Smoking is the primary risk factor for bladder cancer. When Robert came into the room, my heart sank a little. I liked him, but I didn't want to be bogged down with teaching all day. Since I had invested part of a day training him, he would at any rate be more useful this time around.

"Hey Robert," I said.

"Hi Dr. Kork. How are you today?"

"Are you here to practice intubating?"

"Sure, if you'll let me. Good morning, Ma'am." Ruth Faircroft had just entered the room.

Ruth did the pre-anesthetic check ritual, reciting the patient's name and procedure and did anyone have any questions or concerns. When she was done, she said, "Okay Robbie. Let's go scrub."

"What's this?" I asked. "Aren't you on the anesthesiology career path any longer, Robert? Aren't you interested in managing airways?"

"Robbie has changed his elective to urology and is working with me now," Ruth said.

"Well, isn't that peachy," I said, although I was secretly glad.

"Don't be like that Matt," Ruth said. "You know surgery is a more dynamic and manly specialty than anesthesia. Skills not pills, Matt. Do the intubation Robbie and then come out and scrub with me."

"Yes, Ma'am."

"Knock him out, Matt. Chop chop! We have a busy day."

Ruth wasn't wrong. There are really only two operations anesthesiologists do—general and regional anesthesia. The first operation of knocking them out employs a very similar drug sequence every time. Regional anesthesia, or the injection of freezing around nerves, is more creative. It requires knowledge of the anatomy of accessible nerves and facility with the use of an ultrasound machine to visualize them. Regional anesthetics can add 30 minutes to a case, so they are hard to incorporate into a busy list without upsetting surgeons. So, in effect, just one operation.

"He doesn't need to be intubated," I said. "I'm going to use a laryngeal mask airway. Do you want to do that, Robert?" The laryngeal mask was a clear tube that flared into an inflatable, flesh-coloured oval shape resembling a part of the female anatomy. It was pushed blindly into the patient's mouth and sat in the back of their throat, splinting their airway open.

"Come on then, Robert," Ruth said. "There's minimal skill required for that."

Robert and Ruth came back into the O.R. with their hands held at shoulder level and water dripping from their elbows. "I cleared the change with Robert's program electives coordinator, didn't I Robbie? What a cunt!" Female surgeons are the only ones who are allowed to drop the C-bomb. "Have you met that woman, Robbie?"

"No. Thanks for speaking with her, Ma'am."

"You can call me Ruth, Robert."

"Yes Ma'am."

"Well," Ruth said, "she started to tell me about how it would be difficult because there were documents to sign accepting responsibility for giving Robert a good experience, but I didn't let up. Did you use the vaginal airway, Matt?"

"Yes. I don't know why they make it that colour."

"Robbie's a military historian. Did you know that, Matt?"

"No, I didn't. What era are you interested in, Robert?"

"I like them all, with a slight preference for modern," Robert said.

Ruth passed a cystoscope through the first patient's penis into his bladder and the tumour appeared on a screen over our heads. She began carving it out with an electrified wire loop. Since there was a risk of perforating the bladder with carving too deeply or leaving tumour behind with not deeply enough, there was no way Robert would be allowed to participate.

"Did you study military history at the Royal Military College, Robert?" I asked.

"Yes, but most of what I know comes from reading and research."

"Do you know anything about nerve agents?"

"Well, the Germans invented nerve gas in 1938, but they didn't use it in World War II. Interestingly, Hitler himself was gassed in World War I. The Japanese used gas against the Chinese, but neither the Germans nor the Japanese used gas against the west for fear of retaliation.

"The British developed VX and Sarin in 1948. A drop on your skin can kill you in minutes. The Soviets developed binary agents in the 1980s, which they called Novichok or new agent. They were safer to store. There are two components which are inactive until they are combined."

Ruth interrupted. "So, are you meeting any young ladies in our fair city, Robert?"

"A few. There's a singles' bar downtown."

"Anyone who you're serious about, Robbie?"

"I'm still young. I'm not interested in marriage," Robert said.

"Are you a player, Robert?" I asked.

"No sir. I wouldn't say that."

"So, I was in fixing an unrecognized cut ureter in the middle of the night last night thanks to a repeat Cesarean section the previous day," Ruth said.

"Who was the obstetrician?" I asked.

"I won't say the name. It's not the first time. You can look it up on yesterday's list."

"Why didn't you call me?" Robert asked. "I would have come in to help."

"I thought you were commuting here. It was crowded around the table anyway, Robbie. I wasn't in a great mood. I don't care if you're Mother Teresa. If you've been awake for 24 hours, you're an asshole."

"Do you have a place to stay in town, Robert?" I asked.

"Yes, the hospital gave me an apartment in the nursing residence. I've moved in for two months."

98

"It's nice that you have a place to entertain. Okay, call the ureteroscopies for this afternoon in early please," Ruth said to the circulating nurse. "We only have two bladder tumours left. There can't be any delays. I always say please, even if I don't mean it."

We moved on to ureteroscopies. Ruth inserted a flexible scope into the tube between the bladder and kidney, and pulverized kidney stones with a laser into fragments that could be irrigated out. There was nothing that Robert could be allowed to do to help with this procedure either. One misdirected firing of the laser would perforate the ureter. He stared dumbly at the monitor watching and feigning interest.

"Nerve agents were used by Saddam Hussein in his war against Iran in the 1980's," Robert volunteered. "The Americans supported Sadam in that war. Saddam also used them against the Kurds in his own country. Terrorists used them in the Tokyo subway bombing. Is there anything else you want to know about nerve agents, Dr. Kork?"

I couldn't think of anything.

At the end of the day, I went to visit John Hartley again. His nerve stimulator response pattern had normalized, showing that his paralysis had dissipated, but he was still unconscious. I called George Stefaniuk, and we agreed to discontinue sedation and to do a trial of removing John's endotracheal tube the next morning. Extubations are done in the morning so that there is staff around to intervene if the endotracheal tube needs re-inserting.

I picked up the phone and called Richard Tull.

"Hi Richard. Regarding the toxicology on Hana Sato, the case from the Coventry train station—I spoke to the lab director and got him to prioritize it to two weeks. The full tox doesn't include organo-phosphorus insecticides. She said that sending blood to outside labs for that had to go through the Chief Coroner. I think it would be worth doing."

"Was her husband able to tell you anything?"

"No. He's still intubated. We're going to do a trial extubation in the morning."

"Let's see what the initial tox shows. If we draw a blank at that point, we can consider it. I'd like to know what the husband has to say—if you can get him off the ventilator and he's mentally intact. Let me know."

We gathered around John's bedside the next day. He was alert enough to nod his head in understanding when we instructed him that he would shortly be breathing entirely on his own. The respiratory therapist suctioned John's throat and down his endotracheal tube. Then she removed the tube from his windpipe and turned off the ventilator. We held our collective breaths.

"Hi John. Do you remember me?" I asked.

John's voice was hoarse. "My memory's a little foggy, but yes. I met you on the Rocky Mountaineer train."

"I'm Matthew Kork. I am an investigating coroner. I'm terribly sorry for your loss."

He winced. "I overheard that you were the one responsible for saving me."

"No. That was the emergency room doctor, Dr. Hinkle."

"Well, thanks anyway. How is Hana?"

We all looked at each other. Was he in denial? I thought he knew that his wife had died, but of course, unless one of the nurses had let it slip overnight, he couldn't have known. "I'm sorry, John. She's passed away," I said.

John's expression didn't change. "Did she suffer?"

"I don't believe so. She had died by the time the train pulled into Coventry. You're in Coventry General Hospital, in the intensive care unit."

"Was it an accident that we were on the same train together from Vancouver?"

"Yes. I'm not a stalker."

100

"Okay."

"Can you tell me what happened on the train on the morning that Hana got sick?"

"The last thing I remember is coming back to our compartment from breakfast. She wasn't sick then."

"What did you eat? Did you and Hana have the same thing?"

"I probably had breakfast food—bacon, eggs, toast, orange juice, coffee. They served that on the train. She would have had more fruit."

"Did the food taste off?"

"No. I don't think so."

"When did you both start feeling sick?"

"I felt sick after we got back to the cabin."

"What kind of symptoms did you experience?"

"Weak, dizzy, nauseated. Hana didn't tell me she was feeling sick, but she didn't look well. She wasn't one to complain."

"Why did you go to the passenger car and ask to borrow the bear spray from Jack Rielly?"

"I don't remember doing that."

"Do you remember your neighbours in the compartment across the hall from yours? They were a French couple."

"They were on their honeymoon, weren't they?"

"Yes. Do you remember speaking with them on the morning that you got sick."

"No."

"Did you or Hana ever have thoughts of harming yourselves?"

"No, of course not."

"The French couple said someone might have been going through your suitcase that morning. Do you remember them telling you that?"

"No."

"Okay, thanks. I'm very sorry for your loss, John. We're still piecing together what could have happened. Hana's autopsy didn't show her cause of death, but I'm waiting on laboratory results. It looks like you were both exposed to some form of poison. I don't think it could have been food poisoning. The police are going to want to go through some of these same questions. Do you feel well enough to speak with them?"

John glared at me. "I don't know."

After I left his bedside, I texted Branko that John was awake and able to converse.

Chapter 14

Toronto, Ontario

"**M**y bum hurts from playing pickleball yesterday and my wrist hurts," Katya said.

"I know honey," I commiserated. "Pickleball is tough. How did our guests do on the court with you?"

Everybody was playing pickleball at the Rec Centre these days. It looked like a game you would play when you were too old to run around a tennis court and too weak to swing the racquet. It was a sport I felt eminently qualified for. Unfortunately, I had to work, so I couldn't join them.

"Jadwiga's quite good. Jack's already better than I am."

"Well, she's younger. She was a child prodigy on Polish TV, wasn't she?"

"Her mother was a singer on television in the eighties and nineties before Poland joined the EU and became sophisticated. She had Jadwiga on a few times to accompany her. Should I take drugs for my wrist?"

"Were you wanking?" I asked. "Cause you should change hands."

"Ha-ha. No."

"Try some Tylenol. It doesn't hurt your kidneys or stomach."

"In my mind Tylenol doesn't work."

"Remember that placebo effect is 50%."

The next leg of our group sightseeing tour featured a trip to Toronto. I had managed to secure four tickets to a Toronto Maple Leafs hockey game. My brother-in-law had inherited the right to buy season's tickets and I used our relationship to coerce a favour. The team is mediocre, but Canadians love hockey. The tickets for home games are highly sought after and good seats are only available through connections.

We had a full day of activities planned. After dropping Madame Fifi at Summer's house, we took advantage of the morning train to avoid driving in city traffic. Toronto's Union Station is within walking distance of the arena and the landmark CN Tower, which was formerly the tallest free-standing, man-made structure in the world.

I had never taken the elevator to the top to look down through the glass-bottomed floor on the viewing platform and this day would be no exception. I am queasy with heights and I don't see the point. The other three joined the lineup to make their pilgrimage, while I waited at the bottom amongst the buskers, scalpers and pick-pockets.

Next, we hiked along Yonge Street to the Eaton Centre shopping mall for some browsing. Doubling back, we found ourselves in front of Union Station again with a little extra time to kill before dinner and the game. Jack had seen a billboard advertisement for the Hockey Hall of Fame and asked whether it was worth a visit. It was almost directly across the street from where we were standing. Having never been, I said why not.

The displays inside were eye-catching and highlighted the jubilation of victory and agony of defeat. I was enjoying myself wandering amongst the memorabilia and trophies since I was familiar with most of the retired players. Jack was carefully reading the place cards for the displays. The ladies looked bewildered.

"Looks like soccer on ice with more protective equipment," Jack said.

"That's exactly what it is, but nobody watches soccer in North America. I guess you would call it football. Ice is faster than grass, so the games never end nil-nil or one-nil like in soccer."

"We call it soccer too, but we prefer Aussie rules football and rugby league. The only protective equipment the players wear is a headband to keep their ears from getting ripped off. Used to be too many ears on the pitch that players would trip over."

"Well, I've learned something," I said. "That room over there is where they keep the Stanley Cup. Let's have a look."

We entered a domed room resembling a plush-lined vault that contained huge trophies in glass cases. There was a line-up to view the Stanley Cup, the most coveted of all hockey trophies, which we joined and filed past. Jack paused to look at the framed jersey of Paul Henderson.

"Who was this guy?"

He scored the winning goal in the 1972 Summit Series between Canada and the Soviet Union—the most monumental series in hockey history. It was the first time east had ever faced west. The Russians played a possession game, like it was European soccer. We were shocked by their skill, but if they got jostled, they collapsed and faked injuries. The Canadians had never seen such wimps. They mocked and kicked them while they were writhing on the ice.

I recognized a person standing about six feet away, reading the inscription on a lesser international trophy.

"Slava Ukraini," I said.

The man ignored me.

"I didn't know Ukrainians were hockey fans. Are you going to the game tonight?"

He was thinking, still not speaking.

I tried a shot-in-the-dark question, designed to recognize a fellow operative. "Is your buttermilk frothy?"

105

"Yes, but only on Tuesdays," he answered sarcastically in Slavic-accented English. "The Canadians only won because their coach sent Bobby Clarke to intentionally break Kharlamov's ankle."

"Russians only understand brute force. The cops are looking for you."

His face was grim appraisal. "There is a variety of ways this could go."

I took out my phone to take his picture.

"You better watch your back. One of these days when you're not looking—and no lubricant either. Apple in your mouth." He walked briskly away as I took an image of the back of his head and then dialled 911.

Jack came over to join me. "Did you recognize that guy?" I asked.

"Bloody right. That was the guy who judo chopped me on the train."

"Why didn't you kung fu him?"

"It's only for defensive purposes."

"This is 911. What is your emergency?" the operator asked.

"Hi. I have just seen a man who is being sought by the Ontario Provincial Police. He just left the Hockey Hall of Fame in downtown Toronto."

"Who are you? Is this some kind of prank?"

"I'm an investigating coroner."

"It's inappropriate for you to dial 911 in this kind of situation. Please call the Metro Police directly."

"I'm an investigating coroner from out of town. He was involved in one of my cases. I think that the OPP is taking the lead in investigating—"

"Please call the OPP then." She disconnected me.

"Fuck me!" I said into the phone. "I don't know their fucking number. Does the OPP even work in downtown Toronto? I don't think so."

106

"You should just call the blokes in Coventry who interviewed me and let them make the calls. Might save a lot of explanations," Jack suggested.

"Okay. That's what I'll fucking do. The cops here might not even be interested. I don't think that there are any criminal charges against him anyway. Are you willing to swear out a complaint of assault against him, Jack?"

"I don't know, mate. The case might take years to come to court."

"You can use my guest room," I said.

I called Branko on his cell. "Guess who I just met."

"You probably meet a lot of people in your line of work. Most of them are either dead or unconscious."

"I just ran across the guy who judo chopped Jack Rielly on the train in Coventry last week."

"No shit! I thought he would probably be out of the country by now. Where are you?"

"I'm at the Hockey Hall of Fame in Toronto."

"Did you try calling Metro Police?"

"I called 911. They told me I was being inappropriate."

"How long ago was this?"

"Five minutes."

"Well, there is no arrest warrant out for him. It's actually an OPP and an RCMP matter now. You could have told the 911 operator that you wanted to speak with either of them."

"I don't know the case number."

"Okay, never mind. Leave it to me. Thanks for calling. Is Jack Rielly still staying with you?"

"Yes."

"That's good. Keep him around a while longer."

"Did you interview John Hartley?"

"A group of us are going tomorrow."

Katya and Jadwiga had noticed the interaction and came over to join us. Jadwiga looked like she'd seen a ghost.

"Who was that?" Katya asked.

"He was on the train with Jack. He is involved in the coroner's case. I can't really talk about it."

"I've seen him before," Jadwiga said.

"How is that possible? Where Jadwiga?" I asked.

"In Poland, I think. He was a car mechanic. I can't be sure."

We had dinner in Union Station at an upscale restaurant specializing in artisan beer and craft sausages from around the world. We had to wait in a long line before being able to express our preferences. Jack ordered Kranjska from Slovenia and Jadwiga ordered Australian, which wasn't on the menu, so she said she would have what Jack was having.

Although the Maple Leafs never live up to their promise, Scotiabank arena was packed. We had excellent seats a few rows up from the ice. Fans on the opposite side of the rink were passing a giant Canadian flag over their heads making it look like it was floating above them. The game was close and the atmosphere was electric. I noticed Jadwiga counting the ceiling rafters.

"Is this your first professional hockey game, Jack?" I asked.

"Yeh."

"Good as Aussie rules football?"

"Yeh. I think this would go over big in Australia. it's certainly violent enough."

"Attacking players can't cross the blue line ahead of the puck. That's offside. Defending players can't shoot the puck from their end across the red line in the opposite end. That's icing. If you punch somebody in the face, you get a five-minute rest. If you elbow somebody in the face, it's only two minutes. If you hit someone in the face with your stick, that's two minutes, unless they're bleeding. Then it's four."

"Seems fair enough."

"Otherwise, the rules are the same as soccer."

My phone rang as we were leaving the arena. It was Branko. "We need you and Jack to come in tomorrow morning at 10 a.m. Is that good for you? We need you both to look at some images we pulled from the train station security footage. You saw the guys at the hospital. Can you do that?"

"Certainly. Jack, can you make a 10:00 a.m. meeting with Branko tomorrow?"

"Yeh, of course."

The next morning, Jack and I made our way to the police station in downtown Coventry. I parked my car in the liquor store parking lot across the street. Ontario liquor stores generally have large parking lots because they need them.

Just inside the front doors of the station, we were stopped by a glass partition behind which sat a receptionist. Speaking into a microphone, she asked us to state our business. She looked us over and then made a telephone call.

A door opened and Branko emerged, wearing a baggy grey suit that hung off his slender frame. "Hi Matt. Hello Jack. Follow me. I'd like you to meet some people."

We followed him down a corridor into an office that was notable for its clutter and inexpensive furniture. There was a filing tray on the floor, five chairs and a heavy desk that looked like high school teachers' surplus stock. Two men in business suits stood up to greet us.

"Matt, Jack," Branko said, "these are Detective Sergeants Gordy from the OPP and Jones from the RCMP."

We shook hands and exchanged hellos and business cards. Gordy was in his late forties, trim and fashion-conscious. His bleached teeth contrasted with his suntan. Jones was probably a few years older and flabby around the middle. They were both white and clean-shaven.

"That makes three police forces. Why so many?" I asked.

"Since the death of Hana Sato occurred on a train originating in Vancouver, it's a federal matter," Jones, the RCMP man, said.

"The high-level brass had a discussion and decided that it would be a joint investigation, with the OPP taking the lead," Gordy said.

"It's not that we can't do our own murder investigation," Branko said. "The number one concern for municipal police forces is budget constraint."

"The second priority for municipal services is looking effective in the eyes of their city in order to stay relevant," Gordy, the OPP man, said, smiling. "Especially if they are over budget, and the city is entertaining the possibility of firing them and switching over to an OPP or RCMP policing model."

"We'll do most of the work and give Branko most of the credit," Jones, the RCMP man, said.

"Okay," Gordy said. "Have a seat please, gentlemen. We'd like you to look at some pictures." He dimmed the lights and opened a laptop wired to a projector on the desk. "You've both seen the two suspects. Jack, you saw them on the train. Matt, you met them in the hospital. I'd like to confirm that we are talking about the same individuals."

"We met one of them in Toronto at the Hockey Hall of Fame as well," I said.

"That's right," Jones said and perched himself on a corner of the desk. "We want you to identify him."

Gordy projected some pictures onto a greyish-white wall. "These pictures are from the train station security cameras."

The first black-and-white image showed a burly man with a brush cut holding another man, who was bent over, by the elbow, surrounded by other passengers on the Coventry train station platform. The next grainy image was zoomed in on the erect man's face.

"That's him," Jack said. "The guy who judo chopped me and who we saw in Toronto."

"Witnesses on the train said that you exchanged several blows with him. Tell me again why you did that." Gordy scrutinized Jack's face.

"I was defending myself. He had just tased John."

"I see… What about you, Dr. Kork? Is that the guy you saw in the emergency department at Coventry General?"

"Yes, and again in Toronto."

"Are you sure?"

"Yes. He had a mole on his left cheek."

A new colour image appeared on the wall. Jones spoke up. "These next shots are from airport security camera footage. Is this the other guy?" The picture showed a line-up of people with carry-on luggage. In the centre was a man in his forties with a brush cut, wearing a leather jacket. He had a bag hanging over one shoulder and an arrow pointing at his head. The projection changed to a zoomed-in view of his round face.

"I don't know," I said. "When I saw him, he was bent over and had his eyes shut."

"What about you, Jack? Is this the second guy on the train?"

"I didn't get a good look at him," Jack said. "He was sitting behind me."

The cops didn't say anything for a few seconds. Then Jones said, "His eyes look red, don't they, Doc?"

"I think they do. Who were they?" I asked.

"They both entered on Ukrainian passports posing as war refugees. They're probably both Russians using the identities of fallen Ukrainian servicemen," Jones said.

I got up and approached the wall serving as a screen to see the eyes better. "His eyes would look much better in a week. Corneal cells regenerate completely every two weeks."

"The picture from the airport was taken five days after the incident on the train. If it's the second guy, he's gone," Jones said.

"Was he questioned?" I asked.

"He wasn't flagged," Jones replied. "There are approximately 1,000 arriving and departing flights every day at Pearson Airport and up to 130,000 passengers."

"Why wouldn't the first guy have left the country by now?" I asked.

"Seems like he is a hockey fan," Gordy said.

"Maybe he didn't want to leave before getting his job done," Branko said.

"I have a house guest who may have seen him in Poland working as an auto mechanic," I said.

"Who's that?" Jones asked.

"My wife's first cousin, once removed."

"That's pretty unlikely, isn't it."

"She wasn't sure. Could you detain him at the airport if he tries to leave?" I asked.

"He could be held on investigative detention for an hour or two if we have reasonable suspicion," Jones said. "I think we have that much. Any longer and we would have to get a judge to agree to an arrest warrant."

"Do Canadian police keep video surveillance on the entrance to the Russian consulate?" I asked.

"We don't," Jones said. "CSIS probably does. He wouldn't go to the consulate because he would know that. He would meet his contact on a street without cameras."

"Okay, that might be it." Gordy stood up and looked over at Jones and Branko. "Do you have any more questions for these two?"

They both said no. Then Gordy asked, "Did you leave a pair of disposable gloves in Hana Sato's compartment on the train, Doc?"

"Yes. I didn't know where else to put them," I said.

"Please don't do that in future. It confuses the scene," Gordy said. "Okay, that's all, I think."

"The first guy dropped his Taser in the train. Did you recover it?" Jack asked.

"Yes, we got it," Branko said.

"Where would they get a Taser?" I asked. "Are Tasers even legal in Canada?"

"It was a contact weapon, a stun gun, not a Taser," Gordy said. "Tasers shoot darts. They're both illegal in Canada, except for use by law enforcement. It was a brand you can buy over the counter anywhere in the States."

When we got home, Katya, Jack and Jadwiga decided to go for a bike ride while I got some report-writing work out of the way. I didn't know enough about Hana to complete all the questions on the templates. I called the hospital to see if John Hartley was out of the ICU yet and they said yes. That had happened yesterday. He was on ward four-east. If he was poisoned with a nerve agent, I did the right thing leaving my gloves in Hana's compartment.

A HOMICIDAL MANNER, P. Tinits

Chapter **15**

I don't know why he confided in me. Perhaps because I was the closest thing he had to a friend, or because I had known Hana Sato. I drove to the hospital to visit John Hartley. I felt that we had maybe had a moment when he woke up in the ICU. I was curious to hear the rest of his story, and I needed more information on Hana. The Japanese police had informed Hana's parents of her death, but I hadn't spoken directly with them.

When I arrived at the four-east nursing station, I threw a stethoscope around my neck to look official and asked the ward clerk for John's room number. He had the window bed in a two-bedded room. I saw his room mate from the corridor as I entered. "What are you in for then?" I asked jovially.

"Heart attack, Doc," he said.

"Oh, that's too bad. Get lots of rest then. You've made it through the most dangerous time if you're out of the coronary care unit. Hopefully, it was a mild one. I'm here to see your room mate. How are you two getting along?"

"I don't know. I think he's sleeping."

I strolled past the curtain separating the two beds and saw John who had been successfully alerted to my presence. "Hi Doc," he said.

"Hi John," I pulled the curtain the rest of the way around his bed and took a seat. He had looked pale when he was on the ventilator. His face was back to beefy. "You're looking better. How are you feeling?" I asked.

"I'm alive, Doc. That's the most I can say about it."

"You've had a rough time."

"Yes. I miss Hana very much. I can't believe she's gone."

"Tell me about her, if you feel like talking. Tell me how you met her."

He paused to collect his thoughts. "I remember I was travelling in Japan. She approached me in a train station because I was a Westerner. She wanted to practice her English, so I said we should have a cup of tea together. There was a restaurant in the station. When we had finished our tea and were getting up to go, she kissed my cheek even though we barely knew each other.

"That was very forward for a Japanese girl. It was the kiss of a girl waiting for something big, for someone to come and take her away from her small town so that she could start the next phase of her life."

"I had a similar experience when I met my wife," I said.

"She asked whether I would like her to give me a tour. We spent the day together just wandering around gardens and an open-air farmers' market. She offered to make dinner for me, so we took the market produce back to her apartment and she made tonjiru soup."

"What's in that?"

"It's pork and vegetables in miso broth—fermented soybean broth."

"Sounds delicious. I love miso soup."

"We were pretty much inseparable after that. I moved in with her."

"Did that cause a scandal with her family?"

115

"No. She was in her forties and divorced. I only met them a few times. They only spoke a few words of English. We did a lot of bowing and smiling at each other."

"Did Hana work?" This was a question on the coroner's report template.

"She had a dance studio and was also an artist. She did pen and ink drawings."

"What was her subject matter?"

"Pastoral landscapes. Nature as mystical and divine." He seemed to know his art categories.

"They sound beautiful," I said.

"Her death proves that there is no God."

"I haven't experienced the same tragedy as you, but I've come to the same conclusion."

"Or that he hates you," John said angrily.

"Were you stationed in Japan?"

"I told you that I was ex-military, didn't I? Yes, I was stationed there. I was working for military intelligence in Japan for a while. I speak some Russian. Japan is close to Russia."

"Who do you think attacked you and Hana on the train?"

"I don't know, but I can guess."

"Who do you guess?"

"After my government was done with me, they didn't resettle me with a new identity. They said they would, but then they didn't. A guy with a suitcase sat down beside me on a park bench in Maryland. He said they couldn't go to the expense of resettling or guarding me. He said don't go back to your apartment. Then he got up and walked away without the suitcase.

"My name was printed on the luggage tag hanging from the handle. When I pulled the card out from under the plastic, it was a folded list of instructions: *Don't go back to your apartment. Walk away. Start a new life.* I opened the suitcase in a public bathroom stall. It contained new clothes in my correct size—three shirts, two pairs of pants, seven pairs of underwear, one suit jacket, two pairs of sunglasses, a ballcap and an umbrella. In the zippered section of the lid, there was a Canadian and a Japanese passport and $280,000 in cash and prepaid debit cards.

"I took a cab directly to the airport and flew to the Philippines. That was seven years ago. I was travelling until I met Hana and moved here. I was going to look for a part-time job in Coventry."

This was nothing like what I had expected. I was flabbergasted but kept my tone level. "Why $280,000? How did they arrive at that number?"

"I don't know. They used some arcane formula or they thought it would look better on the year-end financial statement to not round up to $300,000. It would look like they were saving $20,000."

"Has Detective Marcovic or any other police officer interviewed you yet?"

"My nurse said that he was coming today."

"He should be hearing this. This interview should probably be continued in a more private setting." The curtain dividing the room in half was hardly soundproof. The policemen whom I had met in the morning should probably have been interviewing him before me. Of course, John's story might all be bullshit.

I got up to go. "I'm very sorry for your loss, John. I'm going to ask Detective Marcovic whether he can arrange for a guard to be posted on the ward for you."

When I reached the doorway, John's room-mate called out, "Don't you wanna check on me as well, Doc?"

"No. You have a different kind of doctor."

"When is my doctor coming?"

"Soon. Use the call bell to ask your nurse."

When I got home, everyone was gathered around the kitchen table eating sauerkraut soup. We had a shop in Coventry that specialized in soup. This one was our favourite. It was sold in frozen card-board containers holding two servings.

"Any left for me?" I asked.

"Sure hon. I made two," Katya said. "Check on the stove."

"Sure hon. Sure hon," Jack and Jadwiga echoed.

There was less than my usual and customary amount left in the pot and not very many chunks of sausage mixed in with the blenderized cabbage. I held my peace and pulled up a chair.

"Seeing dead people today, hon?" Katya asked.

"No, I just had to see a patient at the hospital."

"Jadwiga and Jack are making dinner tonight," Katya said, "Polish bigos."

"Yes," Jadwiga said. "You are making too many dinners for us and spoiling us." She looked very cute. She had brushed her hair behind her ears and trimmed her blonde bangs in a straight line across her forehead, like a younger version of Katya.

"That sounds delicious," I said. "Is it an old family recipe, Jadwiga?"

"Yes. My grandmother, who is very old, also has a very good recipe. I love her because she made bigos for me when I was a little girl. Bigos make me feel like home." Her voice conveyed genuine passion for bigos.

"Do you miss your grandmother a lot?" Jack asked.

"Yes, but we must live and love in the present. Katya, what do you call kapusta in English?"

"Cabbage."

"Yes, it is very close. And sauerkraut is from German. I do not have to make up new words—just mostly mumble."

"Every word is ultimately made up, Jadwiga," Jack said kindly.

"Australians are experts. Listen to the lyrics of *Waltzing Matilda* and try telling me what the song is about," I said.

I noticed a pair of knitting needles with about six inches of fisherman's-knit grey wool fabric suspended from them on the corner of the kitchen table. "Are you taking up knitting again, Katya?"

"No. Jadwiga is knitting a sweater for Jack."

"Winter is coming," Jadwiga smiled mischievously.

"How long does it take to knit a sweater?" I was wondering how long she was thinking of staying.

"You do not have to worry, Matthias. I will have this finished in a week."

"I think it's a great idea, Jadwiga. We're in the snowbelt. Knit lots of sweaters and a baby blanket."

Jadwiga flushed and Katya gave me a stern look.

"I'm thinking of going to the gym after lunch," I said. "Are you interested in coming along, Jack?"

"Yeh all right. Haven't done that in a while. Can you lend me some clobber?"

I remembered this word from my time in New Zealand, where women glow and men chunder as they do in Australia, although not quite as much. "Sure. You look like you're about my size."

"Should we work our glutes or lats or traps?" He was being ironic.

"I was thinking glutes and pecs. What do you think girls?"

"Yes please," Jadwiga said.

"Would you like to come along and oil our bodies?" Jack asked.

Jadwiga laughed nervously. "No thank you."

When we were walking across the parking lot at the Coventry Recreational Complex, Jack asked, "Do you mind if I stay with you a few extra days? I think I might be getting interested in Jadwiga."

"Not at all. Stay as long as you like. I thought I noticed a spark at lunch."

"She's an attractive woman. Doctor too, so she must be smart."

I approached Abby, the clerk in the lobby, and asked about a guest pass for Jack. She told me that since I was such a loyal customer, I was entitled to a free one, and was he interested in joining? When I told her that he lived in Australia, she handed me two extra passes.

As we entered the weight room, Zappa, a bulked-up gym regular, was waving me over. Zappa was in his fifties and had stringy, shoulder-length blonde hair like a California surfer-dude. He was dressed in calico pyjamas and stacking a row of 20-kilogram plates onto a bench-press bar. He had a cane in one hand and was dragging one leg.

"Did you injure your leg, Zappa?"

"Doctor says I have a disk out in my lower back." He dropped the cane on the floor, lay down on a bench and started doing arm presses. "Can you spot me, Matt?"

"Ah, sure." I put my hands on the bar as he hefted it. "Did the doctor say you should be pumping iron with a disk pushing against your leg nerves?"

"He said not to do heavy lifting but to keep active." After ten repetitions, I guided the bar back onto the frame above his head as he was barely able to lift it. He reached down for his cane and pushed himself into a standing position. "I'm keeping active."

"This is Jack from Australia, Zap."

"Hey Jack," Zappa said. "Get used to the cold yet?"

"Yeh, nice kit you're wearing."

"You like it? I sell this stuff. I've got everything on my website."

With the assistance of his cane, Zappa limped over to where a young woman with stars tattooed on the back of her arm was helplessly trying to adjust the resistance on the pulleys of an arm exercise machine. He reached down to the pin in the weight stack and moved it into the lightest position. "It works like this, Amanda."

He pulled on the two handles effortlessly to demonstrate and then hobbled back.

"Yeah," Zappa said. "What's your size? I got these in polka dots, horizontal convict stripes and paisley as well."

"Who's the girl, Zappa?" I asked.

"She's one of the strippers over at Bare Facts. I bring the girls over as my guests so they can keep in shape."

"That's awfully nice of you," I said.

"Yeah, well these kids travel a lot and I try to make them feel at home. And it's their business to look good." Zappa went back over to help Amanda.

"Are you going to invest in some calico pyjamas, Jack?"

"Nah."

We both paused to stare at Amanda's impressively curvaceous bust.

I said, "They might be surgically enhanced, but I don't think so. There's a surgeon originally from Barbados in town who says that a young woman's breasts are shaped like fresh ripe mangos."

"I think they're shaped like tears."

"That's a very bad attitude, Jack."

"Do you think he's rooting the strippers?"

"Zap's happily married. He likes looking at their boobs while he's placing their hands correctly on the weight machines."

We resumed our workouts. I used the weight machines, alternating between arm and leg exercises. There was a heavy bag hanging from the ceiling on a chain in a corner of the weight room. After removing his shoes and putting on leather mitts, Jack kicked and pummelled it into submission.

Branko and his colleagues never had the opportunity to interview John Hartley. Soon after I left, he borrowed some clothes that were hanging in the closet, which belonged to his sleeping room-mate, and walked out of the building. John also borrowed $100 cash from the wallet in the man's bedside table, but left the credit cards.

It was a busy time on the ward with relatives visiting, and the nurses didn't notice him leave. His nurse was on break and, since he had just arrived, none of the others knew him by sight. Branko thought that he couldn't have gotten far with little money and no documents. Security camera footage showed John strolling out the front door of the hospital in tight pants and a Tilley hat.

What intrigued me was his motive for doing this. He seemed to be thinking clearly when I spoke with him. He either wanted to avoid speaking with the police or thought they couldn't prevent another attempt on his life. All of the people involved in the incident on the train, except for Jack, were missing. John and the two Russian Ukrainians had disappeared. Hana Sato was dead.

I didn't tell the police about my visit to John on the ward that morning. They might have thought that I provoked his leaving and was interfering in an official police investigation. Since John was still alive, visiting him didn't fit into my purview as a coroner. They probably should have taken a shorter lunch.

By the end of the week, Jack and Jadwiga were going out bicycling together without inviting Katya. They went shopping for groceries and made more Polish recipes for us, refusing to let us contribute to the work or expense. They were sharing confidences and private jokes. She was doing his laundry. I wondered how long it would be before Jack moved into Michael's bedroom with Jadwiga, or Jadwiga into the guest bedroom with Jack.

I asked Katya whether she had noticed the blossoming romance and whether Jadwiga had confided her feelings toward Jack. She said of course she had noticed. Jadwiga had asked her several probing questions about Jack, what she knew about life in Australia and what the rules for EU doctors were for practicing there. She didn't know whether they were having sex.

Chapter 16

J ack and Jadwiga were actually a pleasure to have in the house. Jack was coming out of his shell. It was nice that he had taken to Jadwiga. She was always cheerful and almost formally polite, expressing gratitude for the smallest of favours. Her mannerisms were delicate and precise. She dressed elegantly and smelled good.

Jadwiga was getting close to finishing the sweater that she was knitting for Jack. Her nimble fingers made the knitting needles clack and the yarn disappear as we sat watching movies to cap off the evenings. The torso was done and she was having him sit for fittings before finally attaching the sleeves. He seemed pleased with the product, but it was too soon to be wearing anything that warm.

We had seen most of the local tourist points of interest together. That only left the faraway ones. As their relationship was evolving, Jadwiga and Jack had been discussing a joint trip to Europe. Jadwiga was keen to show him Poland, and I suppose also to introduce him to her family.

My holidays were done, so I was back to working at the hospital and being on call as a coroner. Not being able to spend as much time with our guests as I would have liked, I volunteered for the shortest operating lists, sacrificing some income in the process. This was not an issue for me. There are no luggage racks on hearses.

I had only a half day of work at the hospital and arrived home around noon. Katya was alone in the kitchen. I asked her where our guests were hiding.

"Didn't he tell you? Jack went to Toronto to see a lawyer this morning. I think it's about his divorce in Australia. He has to sign some more papers."

"No, he didn't mention it. Is he coming back tonight?"

"He'll be gone for a couple of days. He said he wanted to visit some friends while he was there. He rented a car."

"Is he coming back?"

"He didn't say goodbye forever. His suitcase is still here. He has unfinished business with Jadwiga. Is it okay if I leave you with her for an hour or two? I have a thing to go to and then have to run a few errands. Can you make her some lunch? She's upstairs in her room."

"Sure. Are you going to one of your clubs?"

"Yes. I'm going to a Canadian Federation of University Women's meeting. I'm the secretary. I'll be gone about three hours."

Katya left to meet her group of exclusive mature women who valued university educations. The doorbell rang followed by an outburst of barking. Summer was on the front veranda, keeping a respectful Covid-wary distance. The dog ran over to give her a lick and then just as quickly disappeared.

"Hi Summer. Are you having a good day?" I asked, pre-empting her.

"I'm having a really good day. Can I walk Madame Fifi?" She was colour-coordinated with the pink and purple streamers on the handlebars of her bicycle that she had dumped on its side on our front lawn.

"Yes, of course. Don't you have school today?"

"Summer holidays!" She looked at me like I was from another planet.

124

I went to get the dog's harness and leash and to find the dog. After pulling her out from under the geometric centre of the dining room table, I pushed her passively resisting legs through the harness.

When I arrived with Madame Fifi, I saw Jadwiga crouched in the doorway at eye level with Summer. "And which do you like more, art or algebra?"

"I like art and sciences and math," Summer said.

"So, everything! Me too! And was your teacher last term nice?" Jadwiga asked.

"Miss Matheson is so nice," Summer said. "She took us on a field trip to a farm where they had jumper horses."

"That is so wonderful. I love horses too. And what do you like to do in your summer holidays, Summer?"

"I do some dog jumping." Summer took out her cell phone. She swiped and tapped on the screen a few times and then held it up. It was a video of Madame Fifi being led up and over a series of hurdles. She was going at full tilt with her floppy ears streaming behind her. The tallest hurdle was about three feet high.

"I didn't know Madame Fifi could do that!" I exclaimed.

"I set up an obstacle course in my back yard," Summer said.

"No wonder she's so tired when you bring her home. Keep up the good work!" I handed Summer the dog's leash. "Do you need a poop bag?"

"I have one, and don't worry. I'll bring her back exhausted again today." Summer started down the sidewalk with Madame Fifi, her hesitancy overcome, trotting briskly beside the little girl.

"Nice to meet you, sweetie," Jadwiga called.

Summer gave a cursory wave over her shoulder.

"I wonder what Summer will be like when she's grown up," I said to Jadwiga. "She doesn't do anything halfway."

"She will be adorable," Jadwiga said.

125

Jadwiga was already adorable. She had her hair in a ponytail and was wearing a fetching pair of stretch pants and peasant blouse. Katya and Jadwiga had been shopping together.

"You're a prize catch, Jadwiga. How come you're not married up with anyone?"

"Oh, thank you, Matthias. My friends from college are nearly all married now. I have not been so lucky in love."

"Why not? I'm sorry. You don't have to tell me."

"My fiancé fell in love with my best friend. There was a thistle in his kiss."

"That's tough. Your fiancé was a fool."

"Thank you, Matthias. Perhaps I am lucky that it happened before we went to the church to say our vows. I think that they are happy together." She didn't look upset or seem to bear them any ill will.

"Did they get married?"

"Yes. I sat in the back row of the church to see this."

"I'm surprised you would want to."

"They were—I mean they are my very best friends. I was invited but did not go to the reception party afterward. I had no escort to sit with me."

Sadness was creeping into her face. My heart went out to her, as it had gone out to Jack. We needed to change the subject. "Tell me about your life in Poland, Jadwiga. Do you have an apartment? Do you have an office? Do you work in a clinic?"

"Okay. I live with my mother and sister in Gdansk in an apartment. I have completed Medical University of Gdansk in pediatrics one year ago. After that, I was working in the University Hospital clinic as before but for better pay until I decide on a path."

"Did you decide?"

"Pediatrics, but first to travel and see the world. When you have a position, then your patients depend on you and of course you cannot just leave them."

"Unless you're an anesthesiologist or a radiologist. Where have you travelled?"

"We have travelled with my friends by train pass around in Europe to Venice, the Swiss Alps, the South of France, Holland, Denmark and Sweden. I have also flown on Ryanair to Britain with my sister to visit my brother. I spent most of my money doing so. That was a good investment in my becoming more sophisticated." She was wearing an impish look.

"Also an investment in memories. Are pediatricians well paid in Poland?"

"It is enough. I do not care so much about the money. It does not take a lot for me to live. A Polish doctor can earn about 20,000 zlotys per month."

"That sounds like a lot of zlotys."

"Many Polish doctors move to Germany for even more zlotys." This sounded like a reprimand.

"Is medical care free in Poland?"

"All adults must have medical insurance through their work. But if the person has no job, then they must pay. Medical care is always free for children and pensioners. You never think of money when you are a pediatrician looking after children."

I felt like I had interrogated her sufficiently and it was time to eat. "There's some chicken left over from last night in the fridge. Can I make you a sandwich, Jadwiga?"

"Yes please. I will make sandwiches for us both, Matthias. You are having too much trouble for me."

"No trouble. If you make the sandwiches, I'll make a salad. Girls like salad, right?"

"Girls like salad very much," she said.

I pretended to be checking my emails and surreptitiously converted 20,000 zlotys to dollars on my phone. It was about a third of what a Canadian doctor could expect to earn. I commenced tearing and spinning lettuce leaves and chopping cucumbers.

Jadwiga chose a full-length, frilly apron from the apron drawer and assembled ingredients. When she had finished, she presented me with a plate of open-faced chicken sandwiches on dark rye. They were slathered with margarine and topped with sliced boiled egg, onions and freshly chopped dill with a large pickle on the side. She had only one sandwich on her plate.

We sat at the kitchen table together. "Is this enough food for you, Matthias?"

"More than enough. You can have one of mine."

"Thank you so much. We will see. Matthias, you are a doctor. Jack does not tell me about this, but I think he has suffered psychological trauma. What is your opinion?" There was gravity in her tone.

"You know that his son died?"

She looked down. "Yes, Katya told me so."

"Losing a child is the worst thing that can happen to any parent. I think that a majority of parents would sacrifice their own lives to preserve their child's life. They would fight any force of nature, any beast, any human to the death. Jack needs a change of scenery and the passage of time."

"Family and friends," Jadwiga said earnestly. "It is not possible to replace a child, but having more children would soften this trauma. One would feel the loss less acutely if one had a large family. I do not have children yet, but I feel Jack's pain here." She rubbed her lower abdomen with an open palm. She may have winced.

"I believe that your being here has helped, Jadwiga."

"Have you been to Australia, Matthias?"

"Yes, twice. It's very hot. People are generally unpretentious, unarmed and more socially cohesive than in Canada. I suspect it's similar to Poland in that respect."

"How do you mean *unarmed*?"

"They have very strict gun laws."

"Do they have tourist places as nice as Niagara Falls?"

"I don't know whether you'd find heart-shaped beds in Australia. They have surf beaches and an opera house. Following the waterfront in downtown Sydney, you pass botanical gardens, opera house, ferry terminal and then boardwalks lined with restaurants. It's all open to the public. You can hop on a ferry to Manly Beach or drive to Bondi Beach on a Sunday afternoon if you want to try surfing."

"Are the men at Manly Beach as manly and strong as Jack?"

"They are all as magnificently strong and handsome as Chris Hemsworth, but no man is unbreakable."

"I think I will have to go to Australia some day," Jadwiga said. She made it sound like it was only a remote possibility, not likely to be realized.

"It's a big commitment—a 21-hour flight, but I think you should do it."

"Matthias, why did your Estonian father go with a German girl? Did his family not think that he was a collaborator?"

That was a word you didn't hear anymore. "She was Baltic German from Estonia. My parents met in Sweden after the war was over."

"How did they get to Sweden?"

"One hundred thousand Estonians fled their country in order not to be under Russian occupation and terror. People who lived near the coast fled in boats to Sweden and Finland. My father went to Germany with the retreating German army."

"Was your father in the German army?" Jadwiga asked.

"Yes. That's how he learned to speak German. The Russians invaded Estonia first in 1940. The Germans invaded the Soviet Union in 1941 and were initially seen by Estonians as liberators, or at least the lesser of two evils. My father was drafted by the retreating German army in 1944 when he was 15-years-old. Boys caught evading conscription were shot. When the Russians returned, they raped every female of any age from eight to eighty. They were and are swine."

Jadwiga seemed unfazed by these details. She had probably heard many stories like them.

I continued, "She never spoke of it, but my Baltic German grandmother almost certainly was raped. At the end of the war, her husband was dead. She and my ten-year-old mother hiked overland during a week of nights from the Russian to the American occupation zone of Germany to safety.

"You asked whether my father's family disapproved his choice of wife. They didn't know whether he was alive or dead. His mother had been to the central square of Tallinn in 1944, turning over corpses of draft dodgers that the Germans had executed, looking for him. He didn't see any of his family again until he was in his sixties when Estonia regained independence."

"This is where Putin is pushing Europe again," Jadwiga said. "Matthias, if you were in the army and had not seen any woman in months, and if you saw a young woman whose countrymen had killed your friends, would you want to rape her?" Her eyes locked on my face.

"I hope not Jadwiga, but the veneer of civilization is very thin."

Summer returned with Madame Fifi after lunch. She was dangling a warm bag of soft poop, which she dropped into my outstretched hand. Jadwiga borrowed Katya's bicycle to get some exercise and the two of them cycled down the street toward Summer's house. Having gotten up earlier than I wanted in order to go to work, I set my phone alarm for 45 minutes and settled onto the sofa for a nap. I thought I might sleep too long if I napped in bed.

I heard Jadwiga return some time after I had ignored my alarm, and made an attempt to get up to greet her. She graciously told me to enjoy my sleep. I did mange to re-assume a standing position but by that time she had gone up to her room. Katya returned about an hour after that.

"How was your meeting?" I asked.

"It was good. The women all want their thoughts recorded for posterity. I'm a little sorry I volunteered to be the secretary."

"Men don't have a club like that here. A university education doesn't make them special."

"Women are more social than men. Did you and Jadwiga have a nice afternoon together?" she asked.

"Yes, we sat in the living room eating bonbons and discussing our love lives."

"Jadwiga told me that Jack was acting cool toward her. She wondered whether she had offended him in some way. She looked like she was on the verge of tears."

Chapter 17

Two days passed and Jack hadn't returned. I sent him a text asking how things were going. He texted back that he had been taking care of some legal and social obligations and would be returning tomorrow. Katya said that Jadwiga hadn't heard anything from him since he left. Katya wondered whether Jack had given any intimation that there was trouble between them. I said not really but wondered privately whether now that the sweater was finished, it felt too warm.

When I got home from work, there was an extra car that I wasn't used to seeing in our driveway. It was a late model electric vehicle that was obstructing the path to my parking spot in the garage. I parked beside the EV and entered the house through the front door.

Katya was sitting with Jadwiga and Robert in the living room. They were on the loveseat together and Katya was in an armchair. I was more than a little surprised to see Robert.

"Hello everyone," I said. "What's going on?"

"Robert just dropped over to take Jadwiga out for dinner," Katya said.

"Hello Dr. Kork," Robert said.

"Call me Matt. I didn't realize you two knew each other. When did this happen?"

Jadwiga looked tanned and healthy in an outdoorsy sort of way. She had been biking on the county roads a lot. She was wearing a matching necklace and earrings that looked suspiciously like the set I had given Katya last Christmas.

"I met Jadwiga on the bike path beside the canal," Robert said. "I offered to give her a tour of the hospital since we're both doctors, and that expanded into a dinner invitation. You have to eat, right?"

"Several times a day at least," I said. "Where are you going?"

"The Exchange has a fresh oyster bar on Friday nights. We both like seafood," Robert said.

I didn't like the sound of Robert plying Jadwiga with aphrodisiacs when the situation between her and Jack was still fluid.

"Robert knows very much Polish history," Jadwiga said.

"Dr. Kork, did you know that the Russians executed 21,000 Polish military officers and policemen in 1940 on Stalin's order. Basically, all men with a university education, since they were all required to become officers after graduating. They were buried in the Katyn forest in Byelorussia."

That's why we didn't have a club. "I'd heard that. Call me Matt."

"I visited Jadwiga's home town of Gdansk when I was stationed in Latvia," Robert said. "Lech Walesa climbed over the wall of the Gdansk shipyard to found the Solidarity Trade Union. That section of wall is on display in a museum there."

"My mother remembers that. It was before I was born," Jadwiga said.

Robert said, "It's a very beautiful city now, full of tourists."

Jadwiga looked pleased with the compliment. "Yes. On cruise ship days, the city is full of tourists."

"You're a real history buff, aren't you, Robert," Katya said.

"He who does not know history is destined to repeat the mistakes of the past," Robert said.

I'd heard that too. Robert escorted Jadwiga into the driveway and opened the car door for her.

"Is Jadwiga moving on?" I asked Katya. "I thought that she and Jack really liked each other."

"I don't know. She's in a new country and wants to try everything. I don't think they have clarity or exclusivity. Robert's quite good looking."

We went to bed before Jadwiga got back. I left the front door unlocked and listened for her return as if she were a wayward teenaged daughter. Madame Fifi announced Jadwiga's arrival with a volley of barking, after which the dog ran downstairs to greet her. I was glad that she was safely home.

In the morning, I went to the kitchen and made myself a cup of tea. Katya appeared about ten minutes later. "No cappuccino today?" she asked. "You've got that fancy new machine."

"I'm not drinking any coffee today. I was lying in bed and couldn't sleep until Jadwiga got home. After another hour, I got up and had a full meal to eat myself unconscious. I took a Gravol, went back to bed and lay there until it kicked in."

"I heard the dog run down the stairs. I didn't hear you get up."

"Which time? Madame Fifi ran down to greet Jadwiga. She heard me clanking dishes later, so she ran downstairs to see what I was eating. She was waiting for me to give her a handout. She waited for ten minutes and then said, fuck this, and ran back upstairs to bed."

"Madame Fifi never has a problem sleeping."

"I was worried about the love triangle that is developing here."

"It will sort itself out without our interference," Katya said.

"This is not what I had hoped for. What does Jadwiga see in Robert?"

"She hasn't confided. Jadwiga's father was in the military."

Jack arrived back from Toronto that afternoon. He was kind enough to park his car on the side of the driveway opposite to where

I parked in the garage. The three of us welcomed him in the drive-way. I shook his hand and both Katya and Jadwiga gave him a hug. Jadwiga's hug was longer than Katya's. He was wearing his motor-cycle jacket and still had his own rugged good looks.

"Did you extend your Canadian visa while you were in Toronto?" I asked.

"No need, mate. I've still got almost three months left." His voice didn't sound as chipper as before he had left.

"Canada's a big country. I think you should extend it," Katya said.

"How long do you have, Jadwiga?" I asked.

"I have a 90 days' visa."

"So exactly the same," Katya said. "That's nice. You should go walkabouts together."

"I think the Canadian government gave Jack more because they like Australians better than Polish people," Jadwiga said.

"You're equally lovable," I said. "We'll get you some forged papers and you can stay forever, Jadwiga."

"I don't think so I want to stay forever, Matthias. It is too long."

Robert dropped over that evening on his bicycle and asked whether Jadwiga was ready. He was wearing a multi-coloured skin-suit and an aerodynamic helmet. He was outfitted for the Tour de France. I left him standing in the foyer and didn't invite him any farther into the house. Jadwiga appeared wearing Katya's cycling apparel and off they went.

Jack emerged to witness their departure. "Well, I think I'll be pushing off soon, mate. I was just packing my things. Thanks for the hospitality."

"Come into my study, Jack. I want to talk with you. I don't want you to leave yet."

Katya was in the kitchen, cleaning up the dinner dishes. Generally, whoever cooked didn't have to clean and I had cooked that evening. Jack followed me down the hall. I motioned him into a chair and closed the door behind us.

"How did the trip to Toronto go? Did you see a lawyer about your divorce?"

"Yeh. It's pretty much finalized now."

"What do you think it was that broke you and your wife up?" I asked. "Was it a question of marital fidelity?"

"Not that. I don't believe she was ever unfaithful."

"What about you? Sorry, it's a very personal question."

Jack paused. "Just once. What about you?"

"No."

"Tempted?"

"Well, three years ago, I was in a coroners' meeting on Zoom. There were thumbnail boxes for the more than 100 attendees displayed across the top and side of my computer screen. I began scrolling through them to see how many people had their cameras on, to get an idea of whether I should turn on mine. The living, breathing faces of about a quarter of them were visible, with names and home towns captioned underneath. The rest had avatars or nothing.

"I recognized the name of an old flame who I hadn't seen since we were in medical school. She had her camera off. I didn't know that she had become a coroner. She was still using her maiden name, but that didn't mean anything. I considered sending her a personal message in the chat pane, *Hey Roseanne. Do you remember when I fucked you on the kitchen counter that one time? That was fun wasn't it?* Then I thought better of it.

"We didn't part on the best of terms. She might fail to appreciate the humour and file a sexual harassment complaint. I checked back a few times to see if she had put her camera on, but she never did. Perhaps time hadn't been kind to her."

"That's not infidelity." Jack said.

136

"Impure thoughts," I said.

"It's a good thing you didn't send it. Could you love a woman who wasn't beautiful, Matt?"

I thought about that a moment. "The question must be answered hypothetically, since I'm married and don't want to screw that up. If the woman was my mother, of course I could. It depends whether you mean emotionally or physically."

"Both."

"The essence of a person lives in their brain. The internal organs keep the brain alive and the outer layers of muscle, fat and skin account for physical attractiveness. Could I love a brain? Amazon Alexa is nice, but I couldn't love her. Could you?"

"No." Jack had had time to compose an answer to my earlier question. "She couldn't forgive me for what happened to Joshua. We argued over stupid things and neither of us knew how to put on the brakes." He looked defeated.

"You've had a rough go," I said. "Are you serious about Jadwiga?"

"I don't know."

"Why not?"

"My life is full of baggage. Jadwiga and I are ten years apart in age. It wouldn't be fair to burden her with me."

"You could let her be the judge of that."

"It's complicated. Jadwiga and I are very different people."

"You obviously love her. Tell her that and let her make her own decisions about your baggage. You might be throwing away a chance at happiness."

"I think she has moved on to Robert now." His eyes evaded mine.

"They've only just met! You have more integrity than Robert. He isn't anywhere close to committing. He wants to do a specialty, so he'll be in training for the next five years."

"A big part of me died when I lost my son. I can't let that happen again."

"Are you afraid of loving Jadwiga because you might lose her?"

"Yes. That's part of it."

"I think that she loves you. You need to nurture that with her or someone else if you are ever going to recover from the loss of your son. It would be better than living with the regret of letting her go. Who knows when or if it will happen again. She's real and here right now."

Jack's face was flushed. "You should consider writing for Hallmark cards," he said in a monotone. "You said you had three motorcycle accidents. What were the other two?"

"On the day that I landed in Australia, I picked up my rental motorcycle and set off to find my friend's house in Sydney. I stopped at a gas station to ask directions. On my way out, I walked through a plate glass window. I was still wearing a leather jacket and a full helmet but I had taken my gloves off." I showed him a scar on the back of my right hand where the glass had cut me.

"What was the other one?"

"I drove into a cow at 120 kilometres per hour on a country road, trying to keep up with my friend who was speeding. The cow moved into my path. It was like hitting a steel pole with a baseball bat. I flew over the cow and landed on my hands and knees scrabbling along the pavement." I showed him a scar on my right elbow.

"Are you showing me your scars to inspire me with your pain tolerance? You should never get on a motorcycle again."

Jadwiga returned on her bike before dark without Robert. She said she had a headache and was going to bed early. Jack wished her a good night, and he and I stayed up late watching a movie on Netflix on the basement television. I felt that Jack and I had had a moment. I didn't know whether he was reconsidering his packing or had already finished.

The next morning, I came downstairs to find Katya in an armchair, and Jadwiga, on the sofa in the living room. They were sitting, chatting, with cups of tea on the coffee table between them. I got peremptory hellos.

Jack arrived a few seconds after I did. He hesitated on the precipice of the room, then entered. He walked soundlessly across the rug to Jadwiga, paused until she met his eyes and then kissed her once on the cheek.

Jadwiga sat quietly, more of a spectator than a participant, as her complexion changed from cream-coloured to pink to bright red. No one spoke. The quiet was both charged and awkward.

"How's everyone today then?" Jack asked and sat down beside Jadwiga.

Without looking at him, Jadwiga's left hand found Jack's right and their fingers laced together.

Chapter 18

A shaft of sunlight reached my left retina through a chink in my blindfold. I adjusted it to cover the breach, but that only created a new one. It was enough to put an end to my sleep. Taking off the blindfold, I saw that Katya was already up and had thrown the bedroom curtains wide.

"I have the answer as to whether they are sleeping together," Katya said. "Michael's room has been vacated."

Rubbing my eyes, I said, "The world is back on track and unfolding according to plan."

"Do you think I should make up Michael's room?"

"Not yet. There was more room for them last night in the guest bedroom. Jack had done some packing, so his stuff was already out of the way. Michael's room is bigger though, so they may move back in there."

"Wouldn't it have been more gentlemanly for him to sleep in her room? It makes her look needy."

"She offered her honour, he honoured her offer, and all night long he was on her and off her."

Jadwiga and Jack made their appearance in the kitchen simultaneously. There was no mention of their new arrangement, but they were relaxed and unapologetically a couple now. They got their own toast and coffee without prompting and took seats with us around the kitchen table.

They had some news. The trip to Europe was back on. I suppose that Coventry was getting too small for them. Everything that could be accomplished here had been accomplished. They had been looking at flights to Paris, leaving as early as a week from now. They were thinking about renting a camper van and driving to Poland. There were a lot of couples in camper vans on YouTube. Their excitement about this next phase of their journey together was palpable.

Jack already had an open ticket to Europe, which he had purchased before leaving Australia. It was a round-the-world ticket, the kind where you fill in the destinations and make the reservations as you go. Australians never go on short-haul trips as they are so far away from the rest of the planet.

After breakfast, our guests excused themselves to get immersed in internet searches for flights and YouTube travellers' vlogs. Katya offered them her laptop computer as it would have better video than their phones and be easier to print reservations. I think that she was also caught up in the excitement and wanted to be involved.

My phone was ringing. Having my life interrupted was so common as to be predictable. "Doctor, can you take a call to an accident scene? It's a hit and run accident in Coventry."

"Yes." I was on call, so I had no other option.

"Okay, good. Police are on scene. You'll be speaking with a Detective Marcovic. Name of decedent, surname Hammersmith, given name Yuri." She spelled out the names for me letter by letter. "Date of birth 28 September 1952. The address is a self-storage facility at 77 Baseline Road, Coventry, Unit number 15."

"A storage garage? I thought you said he was run over."

"That's what I thought. Maybe he was crossing the street outside. The detective would have the details." She dictated his telephone number to me.

"Okay, thanks."

Before calling Branko, I searched for Hammersmith, Yuri on the provincial electronic medical database. There was nobody with that full name and no other Hammersmiths with that date of birth. Either he was never sick, didn't live in Ontario or dispatch got the spelling wrong.

Branko answered after several rings. He said, "I know you think you've seen it all, but I might have a surprise for you, Matt."

"I don't think I've seen it all. What have you got?"

"A dead guy with four passports. He's been run over—it looks like twice. We're at the You-Store-All storage units on Baseline Road. When you see the police cruisers, you'll know you're in the right spot."

Driving toward the outskirts of Coventry, the sidewalks disappeared and were supplanted by open culverts fronting used car lots, warehouses and junkyards. I found the billboard-style *You-Store-All* sign with a black-and-white police car parked underneath. The lane between rows of adjoining concrete block garages was blocked by several diagonally-parked police vehicles. As I approached on foot, I saw that they were obstructing the view of a body sprawled on the pavement.

Branko was standing off to one side speaking to a uniformed officer. He waited for me to traverse the divide between us. "Hi Matt. You know Hunter. It looks to be a hit and run, no witnesses, but before I say any more, I want you to have a look at him."

The decedent was a heavy-set man with a white beard, dressed in cargo pants, a baggy field jacket and a tan shirt with patch pockets, undone to his waist. He could have been going on safari, except for

142

the fact that he was horizontal. One leg was angled abnormally and there were tire tracks across his lower chest and pelvis.

"Does he look familiar to you?" Branko asked.

"It's John Hartley."

"Alias Yuri Hammersmith. He had multiple IDs in his shirt pocket and a key in his pants' pocket that unlocks unit number 15. I tried it and locked it back up. We'll need to ask a judge for a search warrant—unless you can give us one."

"We're only allowed to issue an Authority to Seize for determining a cause and manner of death, and it has to be specific. What do I write that I'm seizing."

"I don't know—spy stuff. I'll tell you after we have a look inside. Aren't you curious?"

"Yes, of course."

"Great. Thanks."

"I'm not allowed to do it to further a police investigation. He has tire tracks across his chest and pelvis, so, you know, the cause of death is apparent."

"Okay, we'll get a magistrate. The OPP and the Mounties will be here by that time and we'll lose control of the scene." Branko sounded disappointed.

"Can I see his passports?"

Branko handed me a zip-lock plastic bag and said, "Put on your vinyl gloves before you handle them."

The bag contained four passports—American, Canadian, Japanese and Russian. The date stamp in the Canadian passport showed that that was the one he was travelling on. The Russian passport was issued eight years ago and was expiring in 2026. I couldn't read any other information on it because it was in Cyrillic script. The photo depicted a younger beardless version of John.

"The passports all say John Hartley," I said.

"Except the Russian. That one says Yuri Hammersmith."

"You read Russian?"

"A little. Serbians use the same alphabet."

"That's an odd alias." I bent down on one knee to examine the body. He had an obviously fractured right femur. The leg was deformed and nauseatingly floppy above the knee at about the level of the bumper of a truck or large SUV.

"Don't go fishing around in his pockets, Matt. Did I mention he has a handgun in his coat pocket, right side?" Branko asked.

"No."

"I left it for the OPP scene of crime officer. Try to avoid pulling the trigger. There's an extra clip and box of cartridges in the same pocket. I could feel the outlines of some loose ones as well."

"Okay thanks. Do you have his wallet and phone?"

"Hunter has the wallet. About a thousand dollars in cash and gift cards. Two credit cards in Hana Sato's name. No phone."

John didn't appear to have any other long bone fractures. There were tire tracks on his upper and lower torso. His abdomen was distended and tympanitic like a drum. There were two defibrillator pads left by paramedics on his chest, which was bruised, mobile and grating when I pressed on the ribs. His scalp was lacerated where his head had hit the ground. I undid his belt buckle and zipper to expose bruising across his pelvis.

"Can you help me turn him?" I asked. "I want to look at his back."

Hunter pulled on his left arm while I stopped him from sliding. Together we rolled him onto his side.

"No knife in his back," Branko observed. "Hold up! What's that? It's a bullet. Don't touch it!"

Hunter peered at the pavement behind the body. "It hasn't been discharged. It must have fallen out of his pocket."

"Maybe he was fumbling in his pocket for his gun." Branko said.

I stood up. "There are no apparent bullet wounds. There is bowel gas and blood in the abdomen. He was run over by both a front and a rear tire. The tire tracks are too close together to be on the same axle."

"Or the same front tire twice if he was hit and then the car backed up over him," Branko said. "How long ago would you say it happened?"

"There is a little jaw rigor but no lividity. The body is still warm. More than an hour, under four hours, I would say." I knew that an hour must have elapsed in the time that EMS had come and gone and that early rigor took a few hours to develop. "Were there car keys with the storage locker key?"

"Yes, on a separate keychain. His rental car out of Toronto is over there." Branko pointed to a late-model white compact sedan parked down the lane.

"What about a driver's licence?"

"He has a Maryland driver's licence in the name of John Hartley." Hunter extended the licence for me to examine.

"I suppose it would be too much to hope for security camera footage?" I asked.

"Not sure," Branko said. "There is a camera pointed at the entrance gate but not at the individual storage units. We'll try to get any video from today. Hunter's going to hunt that down for us, aren't you Hunter."

"Ha-ha," Hunter said.

"If there's video, look for a big, black SUV with tinted windows and no licence plates," Branko suggested. "That's what Russian hit-men drive."

"Okay then. I'll call the forensic pathologist on call about organizing an autopsy." I pulled out my cell phone.

"We're going to be here a while yet," Branko said. "We'll have to inform the RCMP and OPP cops investigating Hana Sato's death. The OPP ident team is already on the way."

I telephoned the forensic pathologist on call in Toronto to tell him what to expect. It was Ron Rasmussen. He sounded excited because it was finally a real forensic case and not a decomposed, shut-in geriatric or derelict who needed an autopsy for identification. He wanted to speak directly to Branko, so I handed the phone to him.

Branko described the situation to Ron. He discussed sending scene photos, the time of the autopsy tomorrow and who would be attending. Everything had to be precise because with homicide investigations, the forensic pathologist would almost always be called to testify in court. I heard Branko describing the location of the storage facility. Then he handed the phone back to me.

"Are you thinking of coming to the scene, Ron?" I asked.

"I wasn't going to, but now, after finding out more details, I think so. I'll be an hour or two getting there. You don't have to wait. I'll call you tomorrow after the autopsy. Are you going to be available?"

"I'm in the operating room tomorrow. If I miss your call, I'll call you back at the first opportunity." I had never seen this happen before. Even though forensic pathologists often said they liked attending scenes, they never did.

When I got home, Katya greeted me with some sad news. "Jadwiga's grandmother died. She and Jack are flying home to Gdansk for the funeral. We should go with them, Matt."

"Where? To Poland?" I asked, incredulous.

"Yes. She was my aunt. We could do a little travelling after the funeral."

"I'd like to go, but I've just had a bunch of time off, Katya."

"Tell them it's a family emergency, which it is. Tell them, you'll retire otherwise. I've looked up the flights with Jadwiga and Jack and everything, and we have to act fast. You've been missing important

146

family events for three decades, Matthew. I really want to go. I have a feeling about this."

"So do I." The prospect wasn't completely outside the realm of possibility. "It's irresponsible, but I'll see what I can do. Were you close? Have I met her?"

"You met another aunt, not this one. She was 90-years old. She was sweet."

I sent off some exploratory texts and emails to Zach White, the chief of my department, and Ruth Faircroft, the surgeon who was currently in charge of operating room bookings.

Ron Rasmussen called me the next day at noon. "We just finished the autopsy, Matt. The police are here with me. I've got you on speakerphone."

I had to listen intently as Ron's voice was echoing. "Okay. What did you find?" I had my pen poised to copy down the results.

"He had multiple rib fractures, bilateral hemothoraces, bilateral comminuted pelvic fractures, bilaterally lacerated iliac arteries and veins, a lacerated bladder, rectum, liver and spleen and a fractured right femur. The cause of death was exsanguination."

"He bled to death."

"Yes. All blunt trauma. It was likely a high-speed collision. He wasn't shot."

"You put him through the CT scanner?" He couldn't have seen all of this detail with dissection alone.

"We do that with everyone now," Ron said.

"I thought from the tire marks that he was rolled over by both the front and back tires of the vehicle that hit him. Alternatively, a vehicle hit him and then backed over him again."

"It was likely the second option. There were no burns from the exhaust system, and he wasn't dragged along the pavement. Likely an SUV. The big front end knocked him flat and then ran him over.

A car would have launched him over the hood or roof and caused a head injury."

"Not a black SUV by any chance?" I asked.

"I don't know."

"Is Detective Marcovic there?"

I heard Ron say, "Are any of you Detective Marcovic?" There was silence. "No, he's not here… Okay Matt?"

"Okay, thanks."

I called Branko to give him the autopsy result.

He said he hadn't attended because he wasn't the investigating officer. As he had predicted, the case had been taken over by the OPP and RCMP. I read the list of injuries to him.

"No bullet wounds?" he asked.

"No."

"I didn't think so," Branko said. "The cartridge matched the ones in his coat pocket. He was reaching into his pocket when he got hit. His gun hadn't been fired."

"Can you tell me what was in his storage locker?"

"Oh, you know—clothes, Tilley hats, baseball caps, toiletries, mattress, sleeping bag, hot plate, some canned food, and a shotgun. Also, a phone, laptop computer, charging cables and a rechargeable battery."

"So, no real spy stuff?"

"I don't know, but—the security camera at the entrance may have been electronically jammed at the time of the hit and run. It was a wireless system. When it came back online, the lens was covered with dirt."

"Really? So, it was premeditated."

"The RCMP seized the phone and laptop. They're the lead investigators now. Maybe their experts can bypass the password protection with brute force. They have equipment that tries the likeliest and then every possible password. It might take months."

"Couldn't you hold the phone up to his face to unlock it?"

"No. It's a burner flip phone."

"Should I email them the autopsy result?"

"Pretty sure they attended the autopsy. A CSIS officer was also on scene at the storage lockers."

"Canadian Security Intelligence Services?"

"That's right. I gave him your number. He wants to talk to you. Stay tuned."

"Why to me?"

"Cause you're so interesting."

I completed and filed the death certificate, for John Hartley-Hammersmith. The cause of death was exsanguination secondary to multiple blunt trauma. There are five possible manners of death— natural, accident, suicide, homicide and undetermined. The manner of death was clearly homicide. The manner of death for Hana Sato was still officially undetermined.

Chapter **19**

It so happened that three surgeons from Coventry General Hospital were going on holiday at the same time. Operating room bookings were extremely light for the subsequent two weeks. They had been considering asking anesthesiologists to volunteer for days off. This very fortuitous turn of events allowed me to go to Poland.

We weren't all able to fly together on such short notice. The direct flights to Warsaw on LOT, the Polish national carrier, were mostly full. The connecting flight to Gdansk, where Jadwiga lived, was especially difficult. There were three through tickets left on the day before the funeral. There was a single first-class ticket two days later as far as Warsaw. That ticket was only $500 more.

I volunteered to go later because I had to work and I didn't mind missing the funeral. I'd never met Katya's aunt. The alternative would have been connecting flights through Frankfurt or some other European capital to Warsaw with hours of stopovers and possibly missing the funeral anyway. With the extra comfort of first class, there was a chance of actually getting some sleep on the overnight flight.

Eastern Europe was familiar to me, as I had travelled to Estonia several times both pre- and post-Soviet occupation. During the communist era, my cousin asked me, "Is it true you always have bread for sale in the West?" I answered yes. My cousin said, "Doesn't that lead to a lot of waste? We make just enough. Of course, the last people in line may not get any." I said that bakeries sell day-old bread the next day for half price. My relatives had never considered that option. Their jaws dropped. "What! Say that again slowly. We want to write it down."

I drove Katya, Jadwiga and Jack to the airport in Toronto for their overnight flight to Warsaw. Since it was after work, we were fighting traffic all the way. Jack and Jadwiga sat in the back together. I couldn't see their hands in the rear-view mirror, but their hands were most assuredly clasped. Arriving back in Coventry to an empty house was lonely, but Madame Fifi at least greeted me like a long-lost friend.

After making a list of things to do and pack, I spent the night waking up to add things. Michael had agreed to look after the dog again while we were away. Although it would be hard to forget, I woke up to add dropping her at his apartment to my list.

My cell phone rang in the throws of packing the next morning. I had forgotten to turn it off so I wouldn't be disturbed. It displayed a seven-digit number that I didn't recognize. Scammers' numbers usually have more digits, so I picked up.

"Hello Doctor. I believe Detective Marcovic told you that I might be calling. My name is Thomas. You were the coroner for Hana Sato and friendly with her husband. Jack Rielly is currently residing with you. Is that correct?"

"Yes. He's not home."

"Do you think we could have an in-person chat at your house or at the Coventry Police station?"

"When? I'm leaving for Poland tomorrow. Can it wait until after I come back?"

"How about an hour from now? Is that convenient for you and Jack? I'm in Coventry now."

"Yes, I guess that would be okay. Jack left for Poland last night."

"Why would he do that?"

"His girlfriend is Polish. He's going to attend her grandmother's funeral."

"That's unfortunate."

"What would you like to talk about?"

"I prefer not to speak about that over the phone."

Madame Fifi's torrential barking told me when Thomas had arrived. A white Honda Accord with Ontario licence plates was parked in my driveway. A tall, thin man in his forties emerged, took off his sunglasses, tossed them back into the car and strode purposefully up the walkway. He was dressed in beige chino pants and a windbreaker. I opened the front door before he had a chance to ring the bell.

"Good morning. Are you Dr. Kork?"

"Yes."

"My name is Thomas. I work at CSIS. I'm involved with the Sato and Hartley cases now."

Madame Fifi jumped up on his leg, primed for a pat.

"Pleased to meet you. Are you a case officer?"

"An intelligence officer."

"Cool. May I see some identification? She won't leave you alone until you acknowledge her."

Thomas hesitated, patted her shoulder and then handed me a business card from his shirt pocket. Canadian Security Intelligence Service was printed at the top in English and French, the name Thomas Creighton appeared in the middle, and a post office box address and phone number were at the bottom. Anyone could have anything printed on a business card at Staples.

I said, "Come in. How can I help you?"

"Thanks." Thomas followed me into the living room and took a seat in an armchair. He laid a notebook and silver pen on the coffee table. I sat across from him on the sofa waiting. Once we were settled, he said, "Well, you're the guy who raised the suspicion of Novichok poisoning in the Hammersmith case. How did you come to that conclusion?"

"I didn't say Novichok. I said an organophosphorus compound."

"Fine. Organophosphorus. Why?"

"Because he had pinpoint pupils, increased respiratory secretions, wheezing, diarrhea, muscular paralysis and loss of consciousness—all of the classic signs of parasympathetic nervous system hyperactivity. I'm familiar with that because I use cholinesterase inhibitors in my anesthetic practice. Organophosphorus compounds are cholinesterase inhibitors. They're in the same class of drugs."

"Are there any other any poisonings or communicable diseases that can do this?"

"I think not."

Madame Fifi was staring up at Thomas, wagging her tail. "She also enjoys being scratched behind the ears," I said.

He token-scratched and the dog lay down at his feet. "Okay. Let's review everything that happened from the time that you were called to the scene of Hana Sato's death to the present. I want to know everything that stood out to you at the scene, everything that Hartley-Hammersmith told you and what the Russian who you identified in Toronto said."

"I actually met John Hartley in Vancouver in June and travelled with Hana and him by train through the Rockies. The details of my findings from the Coventry train are in my coroner's report."

"Yes, the police gave me a copy of that. I want you to tell me the story in your own words. People often remember new details in the retelling."

"Well, we had lunch together on the train from Vancouver. With a lot of coaxing, he told us that he was a Vietnam and Iraq war veteran. He seemed to be deeply scarred by the experience. He witnessed a lot of carnage. His wife told us that he had won a Purple Heart for bravery."

"That is all true," Thomas said.

"He and Hana were excellent tango dancers. She flopped on him like a rag doll as he piloted her around the floor."

"They were dancing on the train?"

"No. In the hotel before we left."

"Tell me about the rest of the trip and how the Australian Jack Rielly got mixed up in this."

I told him the whole story of how Jack met John on the Pan-Canadian, how I gave him the bear spray and how he in turn gave it to John. Thomas waited until I was done before saying, "That is a series of unfortunate events and outcomes."

"This may be completely coincidental," I said, "but there was a Russian woman in our tour group who stole my prescription eyeglasses and notebook while I was napping in a public area of the Banff Springs Hotel."

"I don't have any opinion on that. It sounds like vandalism."

"There was a retired German diplomat in our tour group. He said his name was Max von Scheffel. His opinion was that she was intentionally messing with me."

"Why would she want to do that?"

"I might have unintentionally insulted her. I don't have any great affection for Russians. Actually, I hate the sound of the language if I hear it spoken. It just grates on me. If I hear it when elevator doors open, I'll wait for the next elevator."

"Your wife's Polish background, isn't she? Can you distinguish Russian from Polish? They're related Slavic languages."

"Yes, I can."

"I understand you interviewed John in hospital after he woke up. What did you talk about?"

154

"I needed background information about Hana Sato for my coroner's report. He told me about her and how much he missed her. He was in deep mourning."

"What else did he talk about?"

"He said that he had been travelling in the Philippines and Japan for the last several years, that he intended to look for a job in Coventry. The U.S. government had given him $280,000 and told him to disappear. Why would they do that?"

"His real name was Major General Yuri Hammersmith, born 28 Sept 1952. Russian mother, American father. He emigrated to the U.S. at age 12. He held a position in U.S. military intelligence as he was fluent in Russian. After the Vietnam war, he became disenchanted and started working for the Soviets, and after the breakup of the Soviet Union in 1991, continued to work for the Russians. They made him a secret major general for his services. It's in the public record now.

"At some point, he switched his allegiance back to the U.S. After he stopped being useful to the Americans, they gave him a new identity and some cash and cut him loose. He didn't get any special protection because he'd worked for both sides. He wasn't worth the expense. He would have compromised people on both sides. Have you told me everything you remember?"

"He liked Canada. He liked Japanese food. Can I ask *you* some questions now?"

"Within reason."

"Is Thomas your first name or family name?"

"It's my middle name."

"Why would he risk coming back to Coventry?"

"He was probably planning on leaving the country and needed his passports."

"Why would he want the Russian passport?"

"Maybe just a souvenir. Or, more likely, he wanted to shred it so that it wouldn't be found after he stopped paying for the storage unit. The management of the facility would open his locker and try to sell off its contents when that happened."

"Has there been any sign of the Russian Jack fought with on the train?"

"The RCMP watches the airports. They don't tell us everything."

"Why not?"

"We don't share everything with them."

"Why not?"

"Well, we don't talk every day. It's done through case management meetings and use letters."

"Could you arrest him if you found him or does he have some sort of diplomatic immunity?"

"We have no powers of arrest or detention. We can mitigate threats if we have prior approval."

"Okay, whatever that means…"

Thomas asked, "Why would this Jack Rielly want to fight with a Russian assassin?"

"He's a karate expert."

"So what! Does he have a death wish?"

"In a way, he does. He feels responsible for the death of his son who was riding on the back of his motorcycle."

"I see… This is a strange case." He opened his notebook and scribbled something for the first time. "I guess it's appropriate that bear spray was used to neutralize a Russian operative. The bear is their national symbol."

"Is there some way to reach you, or do I wait for a knock on the door at midnight?"

"You have my business card, Matt. You can contact me if you remember anything more. Don't share my number around."

I took the card from my shirt pocket and examined it. "Is Creighton your real last name?"

"Why not."

Chapter 20

Gdansk, Poland

I found my seat at the front of the LOT airlines plane. I had never flown first class before. It was quite spacious with lots of leg-room. Instead of three, there were only two seats to a row. Flight attendants were serving champagne. As we took off, I could faintly hear babies in economy screaming as the drop in cabin air pressure pressurized their middle ears.

The woman seated next to me was an unnatural blonde of ample proportions. Thinking I would politely make her acquaintance, I introduced myself. It was then I noticed that she was weeping. She dried her tears with a tissue and said that her name was Aldona. While I was wondering whether I should attempt to console her, she apologized and explained the reason for her grief.

She was flying to Poland to bury her father who had died unex-pectedly. She was a travel agent at an agency in Toronto catering to Polish speakers. She looked to be in her middle forties. She had an accent, so I asked whether she had been living in Canada long. She answered, for the past 25 years. She had moved to Canada to get married.

Both my and Katya's parents had some weird uncles who had married gold-digging, mail-order brides from Eastern Europe. They wanted young pretty wives, who spoke fluent Estonian, or in Katya's case Polish, but didn't have modern ideas. This was very difficult to find in Canada.

I innocently asked how old her husband was. Her husband was in fact an older gentleman, but she wasn't with him any longer. She had divorced him and married the husband of her employer at the Polish travel agency. Naturally, she stayed with her first husband long enough to get Canadian citizenship.

"You can think what you like. I was already divorced for three years," Aldona said.

The meal was served. It was a smoked sausage and pasta dish that was good but not fancy. We ate in silence. I was done talking with her and looking forward to sleeping.

"Why are *you* going to Poland?" Aldona inquired.

"I'm trying to learn some Polish."

"No. You are looking for something else. A young woman." Her verdict was absolute.

"This is my first time in first class. I thought the food would be better."

"No. This is a small thing," she said. "The main thing is that the plane is safe."

I raised the footrest of my chair, arranged my pillow and put on my blindfold, but I couldn't sleep. It wasn't comfortable or I wasn't sleepy enough. The programing on the screen in front of me was in Polish. I asked our flight attendant about it and was given a laptop DVD player and headphones.

After watching Tom Cruise scaling skyscrapers for a while, I looked over and saw that our flight attendant had passed out in a vacant seat with her legs sprawled apart. It had been the only remaining empty seat.

"She is not feeling well," Aldona said.

I was immersed in the film when Aldona suddenly gripped my arm and said, "Did they announce an emergency landing?" There was terror in her eyes.

"No. I don't think so. I was watching a movie. Did you dream it?"

"No. They said it."

My heart was racing. This wasn't the way that I wanted my life to end. I noticed that our flight attendant was still passed out, so that was reassuring, but she could have fainted from the stress of the situation. Desperately looking around the cabin for the second flight attendant, I spotted her serving whiskey and soda to someone. She told me that nothing was wrong.

Returning to my seat, I relayed this information to Aldona, who didn't seem completely convinced. I looked longingly at the seat in which the slumbering flight attendant was sprawled, wondering whether she would trade. During the night, I woke up to find Aldona's arm slung over me in a gesture of friendship. There was champagne on offer again in the morning, as befitted a first-class experience.

After passing through customs, I took the train to Warsaw Central Station and found the track for the train to Gdansk. The train ride through the outskirts of Warsaw featured concrete high-rises and Soviet brutalist architecture. That is generally the way in any ex-Soviet country. The historic old city districts built before 1939 are beautiful. Anything outside of that is shit. I passed out for the three-hour ride to Gdansk.

In terms of getting over jet lag, it's supposed to be better to tough it out after an overnight flight and not to lie down until a normal bedtime. I'd had a nap on the train, so that's what I did. I texted Katya when I arrived in Gdansk and took a cab to Jadwiga's apartment where she, Jack, her sister, mother and Katya were waiting with a late lunch.

Jadwiga's mother Ludmila, who was Katya's first cousin, seemed formal and reserved. We weren't close and it was only one day after her mother's funeral. I gave her my condolences, which Katya translated. She spoke very little English, but encouraged Katya to tell me to please eat more because she would otherwise have to throw it out anyway. She smiled approvingly when I followed her suggestion.

I very much liked Jadwiga's sister Diana, who was outgoing and touchy-feely and laughed loudly at my description of my misspent night on board LOT airlines. Diana was a year younger than Jadwiga. She looked like she enjoyed food and drink and would be fun at parties. I told her that there was a barbeque sauce named after her in Canada and promised to send her a bottle along with my salmon recipe.

Jadwiga and Jack were pretending that they weren't sleeping together. Of course, they weren't fooling anyone, but Jadwiga had moved back in with her mother and sister while Jack lived in the same hotel as us two kilometres away. I suppose this still allowed them to slip away for an afternoon delight.

Katya, Jack and I took the tram to our lodgings, which were on the edge of the Old Town. It was a new, made-to-look-older, four-star hotel. There was no elevator, so I dragged my luggage up the flight of stairs. With the only preliminaries being brushing my teeth and arranging my pillows, I collapsed on the bed into oblivion for the next ten hours.

Warm weather was forecast for the next few days. I pulled on shorts and a T-shirt in the morning although, in my age bracket, it's primarily Americans who wear shorts in Europe. I didn't want to be mistaken for one, but my comfort was more important than blending in with the locals. Jadwiga joined us for breakfast in the hotel restaurant, her honour seemingly intact.

We had planned to meander through the Old Town, which is the highlight of Gdansk. I had loaded my backpack with a water bottle, sunscreen and a brolly, which still left room for any souvenirs we might buy. We strolled along the Matlawa River beside colourful six-story buildings with high, peaked roofs as a foursome.

"This is gorgeous," I said.

"There is so much history here," Jack said.

"Yes, thank you. It is very nice," Jadwiga said. "It is all fake. Russians and Ukrainians bombed the Old Town in World War II and it burned 90%. It was built back in 1950s and 1960s."

"Didn't it also get damaged when Germany invaded Poland, Jadwiga?" Jack asked.

"Yes, this is where Hitler started World War II to get return of Gdansk to Germany. Mostly Germans were living here. Then it was called Danzig."

"Gdansk is also the home of Lech Walesa and the birthplace of the Solidarity trade union, isn't it, Jadwiga?" Jack asked.

"Yes, my father knew all the history. There is very much history, very much fighting, struggle and sadness here. For now, everything looks happy, but we remember it."

We turned a corner and walked over the cobblestones of Dlugi Targ, the main walking street, to Gdansk's central square. The perimeter of the square was occupied by the city hall, a large church, museums and coffee shops. Being Saturday, there was a busy farmers' market with lots of locals and tourists.

The most imposing buildings in European historic city centres are usually the churches. The massive front door of the Basilica of the Assumption of the Blessed Virgin Mary was unlocked, so we went in to have a peek. They were charging an admission fee to go past the alcove, so I craned my neck to see the ornate walls and ceilings for free.

Jadwiga provided us with some historical perspective. "The roof of the church burned away during the war. Then, the soldiers of the Soviet Union dug up the floor of the church hoping to find rings and gold teeth from the corpses buried there."

"Your father did a thorough job with his history lessons," Jack said.

"Thank you. I am afraid that for Polish people, history is a national obsession," Jadwiga said.

"Our history in Australia only goes back about two hundred years. Would you like to hear about the first shipment of convicts landing at Botany Bay in 1788?"

"In my humble opinion churches are all very similar," I said. "I think I've seen the best part for free. What does everyone think of grabbing a camp-o-chino on the square?"

"Sounds brilliant," Jack agreed.

We did an abrupt about-face to retreat from the church and were jostled by an onslaught of new arrivals. I heard, "Hello Mister." The accented voice was familiar.

I turned to have a look. "Hello Aldona. How are you?"

"I am very good. I am here to talk to the priest."

"About your father's funeral?"

"Yes. It was yesterday in this church. I am here to give him some money."

"I'm sorry for your loss, Aldona. This is my wife Katya and my friends Jack and Jadwiga."

"I am happy to meet you. So, you were not here to look for a woman."

"No. Jack and Jadwiga are visiting her parents, and Katya and I are helping."

"I think Jadwiga and Jack are lovers," Aldona said.

Looking over at them, I could see they were holding hands. Jadwiga was blushing.

"They are here to get married," Aldona said. "I can help to make the arrangements."

"Are you interested, Jack?" I asked.

"Yes. I know the priest and my sister has a marriage agency," Aldona said.

Jadwiga was blushing more. Jack asked, "What's a marriage agency then?"

"My sister has Armenian, Bulgarian, Romanian, Russian and Ukrainian girls who need to marry a husband. She also makes arrangements for many weddings here and in Warsaw."

I noticed that the list of nationalities was in alphabetical order. "What about Polish girls?"

"Yes, there are not so many now. She is a wedding planner for the Polish girls." Aldona opened her purse and pulled out a calling card. She strode over to Jack with the card in her outstretched hand and a sugary grimace. He accepted the card and tucked it in his shirt pocket.

We wandered along the rows of market stalls in the central square. Jadwiga and Jack paused to buy some smoked meat. There was a lot of meat but also cheese, berries and large yellow fungi with fronds that looked like hands.

"I certainly wouldn't eat any of those if I met them in a forest," I said. "What are they, Katya?"

"They are chanterelles and they're delicious. When I met my grandmother here for the first time, she made me a whole meal of them. She picked them herself. That was during communist times."

"She was probably giving you the best that she had."

Katya was attracted by a display of open-face, raw herring on rye sandwiches. Each piece of fish was sitting on a beet slice and topped with dill. There were plenty of wasps hovering over and on the food. The vendor seemed unbothered and reached through them to pick up the sandwich Katya was pointing at.

"My mother used to make these. Aren't you having one?" Katya asked me.

"I don't eat fish before noon." We found an empty table and I watched her take a bite. "You're getting the authentic experience," I said and snapped her picture.

"The rye bread is fried." She was in heaven.

Jadwiga and Jack joined us with four cappuccinos and almond croissants. We stretched our legs and let the sun warm our faces. An anemic-looking busker with a violin was doing a superb rendition of Sting's Fragile. When it was done, I went over to drop a few euros into his violin case and compliment him on his playing.

There was a small blue-and-yellow flag on his speaker. It prompted me to say, "Slava Ukraini," to which he responded, "Thank you," in English. We spoke for a few moments and I asked about his path to Gdansk.

Returning to the table, I said, "He's Ukrainian. I guess he's a draft dodger—not that I blame him. A talented musician like that shouldn't be cannon fodder. He and all the market vendors spoke to me in English. How do they know I'm not a local? Is it my clothes?"

"Your body language shows optimism for the future," Jadwiga said. "I think in Canada and Australia, you do not have to worry about Russians killing you."

"The world keeps reinventing itself," I said. "One year it's Germans and Japanese killing you, the next it's Arabs and Russians."

"In Oz, we call them all Australians," Jack said.

Jadwiga stretched her arms in the sunlight. "That sounds lovely."

We finished our coffees and got up to go. Hoisting my pack over one shoulder, I felt a sudden pain in my lower neck. "I think I've just been stung by something." I reached back to rub the affliction.

"There could have been a wasp under the strap of your back-pack," Katya said.

"Yeah. There are a lot of wasps around." I could feel a nagging discomfort where the strap was rubbing and shifted the pack to the other shoulder. "Or I strained my neck carrying the backpack. That could be what it is."

The plan for the next two days was for Jadwiga to introduce Jack around to various more of her relatives. I imagined that he would be sitting on their apartment living room couches waiting for translations of conversations with a smile frozen on his face. That didn't interest me much. Katya had already had two days of quality time with them, so we planned to do some touring on our own.

Lounging on the bed, I used the hotel Wi-Fi to research local points of interest and check my email. The toxicology report had come back for Hana Sato. I accessed it on the coroners' web site by entering my password and a second numeric code sent to my cell phone. Her toxicology was negative for every narcotic and everything else.

I went into the bathroom where Katya was getting ready for bed. "I don't know if I can sleep yet. It's only 4 p.m. in Coventry," I said. "The toxicology on that Japanese lady who died on the train was negative. I had a minor difference of opinion with the pathologist. He thought it was a narcotic overdose."

"You're always right, aren't you, hon." Katya was smiling in the mirror.

"Well, I was wrong once. I thought I had made a mistake, but I was wrong about that. Do you think it matters that I used hotel Wi-Fi to access the encrypted coroners' website?"

"I don't know."

"Would it have been more secure if I had used the data on my cellphone?"

"I don't know." She sounded sleepy.

Angling my body to look at my back in the bathroom mirror, I could see a red welt with a black centre overlying my right trapezius muscle. I asked Katya to take a picture with my phone. It looked like the centre was dried blood. "I guess I was bitten after all," I said.

166

After lying in bed for a while, I opened my eyes to see Katya's eyelashes rimming the soft curve of her cheek a few inches away. The regular heave and sigh of her breathing told me that she was deeply asleep. She had returned to the country of her ancestors and re-acclimatized to the local time zone. That one of us had was comforting.

Chapter 21

Katya and I rented a car from a rental agency in the hotel to explore the environs. We spent the day in Sopot, a pretty beach town with therapeutic spa hotels offering curative mud, vapours and other medically proven technologies. I had booked one night at the Sopot Grand Hotel. We had a cup of tea looking out to sea in their five-star restaurant and strolled through the manicured gardens to the beach.

After spending a few hours basking and swimming in the brisk Baltic waters, we browsed shops on the pedestrian Bohaterow Monte Cassino Street. When we stopped to read a restaurant menu, the owner, who was standing outside, demanded, "What are you looking for?" The question was open to several interpretations. Logically, because you posted the menu.

Drawn to a kiosk by the smell of cooking onions, dinner was two sausages, split lengthwise, fried and all-dressed on rye. We munched prune-filled, chocolate cookies from a package for dessert as we gawped at expensive summer homes on the side streets. Back at the hotel, we detoured through the casino to see people who thought that determining their financial fate with a coin flip was entertaining. It was fancy but too small to attract any James Bond look-alikes.

The next morning, we drove to Malbork Castle, reputedly the largest brick castle in the world. It is fully restored and steeped in history. Like most of this part of the world, several nation-states had claimed ownership. War and the vicissitudes of politics moved it ultimately from German to Polish hands. Malbork is only 150 kilometres from Kaliningrad, Russia to the east.

We saw Jack the following day for lunch back at our hotel. He had some news.

"Jadwiga and I are getting married. Your friend Aldona's sister is booking the church and the reception hall. There was only one opening in the schedule, so we grabbed it."

"Congratulations!" we exclaimed simultaneously. "When is the wedding?"

"Next Tuesday. I'm just on my way to choose some centrepieces for the tables and things with Jadwiga. You're welcome to come along."

"Wow! This is sudden and also mega. I'm so happy for you both," Katya said.

"We wanted all of Jadwiga's family to be able to attend. We're going to do it again in Australia for my side. You fly home Thursday, don't you?"

"Yes, so the timing works well for us," I said. "You might not be able to fill the pews of that giant church with wedding guests."

"We didn't get St. Mary's, but there's a smaller church that's available."

I was thinking that Aldona did a bait and switch to get her sister some business.

"I'll need a best man, Matthew."

"If you're asking me, I'd be honoured, Jack. I didn't bring a suit. Do you know whether they do matching, powder-blue tuxedo rentals in Gdansk?"

"Thanks, mate. Aldona's sister Agnies said that she can arrange all that. She gave me the address of a tuxedo rental shop. I want what you and Katya have." He said this solemnly and I was flattered.

"Have you given any thought as to where you're going to live?" Katya asked.

"Jadwiga says she wants to live a peaceful life away from conflict and Russians in a country built by convicts."

After lunch, Jack, Katya and I took a tram to Jadwiga's apartment to attend to wedding details. Jadwiga was wearing blue jeans and a white T-shirt. She was flushed and sporting an expensive-looking new diamond solitaire ring on the fourth finger of her right hand. She put her arms around Jack with her breasts brushing his chest and kissed him lightly on the lips. The two of them settled together on a corner of the living-room sofa speaking rapidly, oblivious to everyone else.

After a few minutes, Agnies, the wedding planner, arrived. The family resemblance to Aldona was apparent. She was an impeccably dressed, middle-aged woman wearing heavy facial bronzer and odd pencilled, high-arching eyebrows like a surprised mannequin. She spread photo albums of options for decorations and floral centre-pieces on the coffee table and made recommendations for caterers, musicians and wedding cakes. The conversation was primarily conducted in Polish, with the occasional English translation. Jack was heavily involved, but I had nothing to contribute beyond generally agreeing with the majority opinion on everything.

After Agnies left, Ludmila provided a light supper. Katya and I walked the two kilometres back to our hotel over sidewalks that gave way to cobblestones. Although I had been physically there, I asked Katya what I had missed.

"Jadwiga's sister is going to be the maid of honour and her brother will be a groomsman," Katya said.

"I think I caught that Jadwiga asked you to be a bridesmaid. Is that why you were all teary and hugging?" I asked. "You weren't translating a lot of things."

"Yes, I'm a bridesmaid! I couldn't tell you everything because it might have cheapened it to repeat it over and over. Jadwiga said that Jack's proposal was terribly romantic. It happened in our hotel. He got down on one knee and said that he wasn't worthy of her, but that he would do everything in his power to make her happy for the rest of their lives. She didn't think that he would have had time to purchase a ring, but when she accepted, he produced a diamond solitaire from the front pocket of his jeans."

"She accepted him right away?"

"That's what she said. I can't believe how short the engagement is going to be—just a few days."

"No shorter than an arranged marriage in India," I said. "She was engaged once before and didn't consummate fast enough. She told me that her best friend stole her fiancé."

"I know that she has had her heart broken. Hopefully Jack is as solid as he seems."

"They have both had their hearts broken."

"It didn't take as long finalizing details today because they were already in place from Jadwiga's first engagement," Katya said.

"I haven't met any father figures. I get the impression that Jadwiga's father is deceased. Is that true?"

"Yes, he died tragically in a car accident. Don't say anything, but some of Jadwiga's family believe it was suicide. He drove over an embankment into a ravine on a clear, sunny day."

"What did he do for a living?"

"He was a military officer. He might have had a drinking problem."

We reached our hotel and climbed the flight of stairs up to our room.

I threw myself onto the bed to get my aching feet elevated. "So, what kind of presents do people give at Polish weddings?"

"Traditionally, it's envelopes stuffed with cash."

"Isn't that crass?"

"It's traditional here. It's also what they need to pay for the five-course meals and open bar."

Something on the night table that caught my eye jolted me. "Katya, look at this."

"What is it?"

"Look at what's on the night table."

"Those are your glasses, aren't they?"

I picked them up and put them on. They were my prescription. "These are the glasses that I lost in Banff!"

Katya paused to digest. "What do you think it means?" She sounded worried.

"I think it's a warning. It's like what the German guy described in Banff—Max von Scheffel."

"Maybe it's time to go home."

"We have to stay for Jadwiga's wedding," I said. "I could report it to my contact at the RCMP, but what good would that do?"

"Tell him about it anyway. You must be under some kind of surveillance."

After our meeting in Coventry, I had entered Sergeant Jones' contact information from his business card into my phone. I brought up his number and texted: *My eyeglasses and notebook were stolen from me at the Banff Springs Hotel last June. The glasses have turned up on a night table in my hotel room in Gdansk Poland. Should I be worried?*

Surprisingly, it was Thomas who had texted me when I checked my phone the next morning. It read, *Your wife might be playing a joke on you.* Ten minutes after the first text, he had sent another one. *Contact me when you get home please.*

We gathered at the church for the wedding rehearsal on the day before the wedding. It was the church that Jadwiga's family attended. Jadwiga's mother Ludmila smiled uncertainly as she shook hands with everyone. Although she had been a singer on television, she seemed shy. Jadwiga's sister Diana gave me a bear hug and introduced her brother Wojtek, whom I'd met but didn't remember.

The priest, looking very saintly, called the meeting to order in Polish and broken English. Ludmila took a seat in the front pew, comfortably in the bosom of other smiling relatives. The priest showed the members of the wedding party where to stand and issued last-minute instructions. I noticed that Jadwiga was saying *no worries* a lot, but everyone says that now.

After the rehearsal, Jack was no longer allowed to see the bride. The women, who were in high spirits, bade us farewell and went off to drink brandy.

Wojtek approached us. "How are you enjoying Poland, Matthias?"

"Very nice. Katya and I visited Sopot and Malbork. Both bardzo. Very nice twice. We were only one hundred kilometres from the Russian border and were considering paying a surprise visit to Kaliningrad. Is the border very heavily defended?"

"It is now," Wojtek said. "It used to be just a formality. Prior to World War II, Kaliningrad was the German city of Königsberg. After the war, it was incorporated into the Soviet Union. It is named after Mikhail Kalinin, one of five signatories to the order to execute 25,000 Polish nationalists in the Katyn Forest. Would you like to go to a cabaret on your last night as a bachelor, Jack?" In Europe, cabarets are strip clubs.

"In the 1990s, my Estonian cousins took me to a strip club in Tallinn," I said. "The strippers were all Russian. They said that no Estonian girl would ever do that. One cousin had also been to a strip club in Helsinki, where the patrons said that no Finnish girls would ever do that. It was only Estonians and Russians."

"Everyone needs someone to look down on," Wojtek said.

"Thanks. I have to beg off," Jack said. "I think I might have jet lag or a bug. Can you give us a lift back to our hotel?"

Wojtek gave Jack a sympathetic look. "No worries."

We walked through the dark parking lot with Wojtek leading the way to his car.

"I think I might pass out, mate," Jack whispered. He wasn't walking very well.

I could see him better when Wojtek opened the car door and the dome light came on. He looked pale, possibly greenish. I helped him into the back seat and put my finger on his radial artery pulse, assuming the airplane doctor role without waiting to see whether anyone else would volunteer. I said, "Put your feet up. Lie back."

Taking a seat beside Wojtek in front, I said, "There was a lot of standing during the rehearsal, Jack. Did you get dinner?"

The hotel was only ten minutes away. "Okay, see you tomorrow at your funeral—I mean wedding, Jack," Wojtek said when he dropped us.

I helped Jack into the hotel lobby and told him to put his feet up again on a chair. He did as he was instructed. There were no Germans around to prevent him.

"Do you think I'm doing the right thing?" His voice was urgent and his eyes searched my face. It was obviously a case of nerves.

"Absolutely. Jadwiga's a lovely, intelligent woman. You're lucky to have her."

"I know."

"You're overwhelmed by all the foreigners."

"The priest took us into his office and made me promise that any children that result from our union will be raised Catholic. It was a condition for his doing the ceremony."

"It's okay to lie to priests. She is your chance for happiness."

"Thanks mate… We could just have a drink in the hotel bar."

We went to the bar where Jack ordered some soup and toast like a convalescent.

Chapter 22

In the history of women and men, men and men, and women and women, nothing is more wonderful than romantic love. The quickening of the pulse when together, the longing and heartache, the hours-long, late-night telephone conversations when apart. It is commonly the precursor to an alliance of minds and bodies, and the making and rearing of babies. For the half of marriages that don't end in divorce, it evolves into a life-long friendship leading to a dotage of marked special occasions, visits with children and grandchildren, and so on.

On the day of the wedding, rather than divide the church down the middle into friends of the bride and friends of the groom, people were instructed to sit anywhere. Jack was outfitted in a white dinner jacket. Wojtek and I were wearing black. Jack had a red rose in his lapel and we had white ones. We stood at the front of the church with the priest, waiting for the bride.

The church choir broke into song and Jack smiled expectantly. He seemed to have gotten over his jitters. There was a hush in the church as Jadwiga entered, arms linked with her uncle, and then the organ burst into a full, vibrant wedding march. A miniature-Jadwiga flower girl danced ahead of them to approximately half-way down the centre aisle scattering petals from a basket. Then, she broke into a run and Wojtek scooped her into his arms.

"My daughter," he said.

The couple promenaded deliberately toward us at the altar. Jadwiga looked radiant. She was wearing an elegant white off-the-shoulder gown with traditional red floral embroidery below the bust and down one side of the skirt. A sheer white tulle veil fell from her blonde hair to her shoulders.

"She may be the most beautiful bride I have ever seen," I said to Jack.

The priest recited a traditional Catholic wedding liturgy in Polish with some English asides. At the appointed moment, I handed Jack the ring, which he placed on the fourth finger of Jadwiga's right hand beside her engagement ring. It was done and very impressively for such short notice.

There were 30 minutes of mingling and photography on the church steps and in the gardens. The reception took place in a hall in the church basement, where the bride and groom were greeted with bread, salt and vodka. A giant, eye-catching, spikey wedding cake in the shape of a tree held place of honour on a table at the front. The floral centrepieces on the dining tables were accompanied by large vodka-bottle centrepieces.

I pointed toward the cake. "Hey Katya. Looks just like our wedding. How do they make that again?"

"Sekacz. Each church has a group of ladies who know the secret. If they told you, they would have to kill you."

"So, wire coat hangers?"

"I heard that they make it on a giant rotating spit."

"Since you can't tolerate alcohol, can you swish and spit the vodka when it comes time to toast the bride?"

Katya laughed out loud. "Pregnant alcoholics aren't allowed even a drop."

"It would be funny though…" In my mind's eye I pictured the shock and dismay of the wedding guests.

"They would have me arrested."

"Does Wojtek speak with a British accent?"

"Yes indeed. He went to university in England."

What happened next took me by surprise. Ludmila's mother took the microphone and sang a pitch-perfect, beautiful version of Ave Maria. When it was done, I noticed Wojtek and his wife were standing off to one side beside a display of family photos. I went over for a chat. "Your mother is very talented," I said.

"Maybe her best one ever. She's caught up in the moment, as are we all. This is my wife Maja."

"Pleased to meet you. You have a beautiful daughter. Katya tells me you went to university in Britain, Wojtek."

"Yes, *old bean*. It was free before Brexit, while they were part of the European Union."

I presumed that the *old bean* was ironic. "How did you find living in Britain?"

"I think, on average, they smile more than us," Maja said. "If you smile at strangers in Eastern Europe, people think you're an idiot."

There was a large portrait on an easel of a military officer in an olive-green dress uniform with a green necktie and a peaked cap. "Is that your father?"

"Yes. That's daddy," Wojtek said. "He's been gone for five years now."

"If you don't mind my asking, what happened to him?"

"He was in a car accident. They say he was intoxicated, but I don't believe it. He didn't drink during daylight hours."

"Do they do blood alcohol levels in Poland?"

"Of course, Matthias, but the petrol in the engine had caught fire. His foot was jammed on the accelerator by the collision. All that remained was a blackened metal car frame with a charred mummy inside."

"What are some of the best things that you remember about him, Wojtek?"

Wojtek's face softened. "He listened to my opinions. We played football together."

Katya and I were seated with the bridal party at the head table. Despite having no stage fright, Jadwiga's mother spoke little and only in Polish. There were five courses of meaty pierogies, cabbage rolls and stews with the only concession to vegetarians being pickled cucumbers, which served as the salad course.

Katya said, "When I was here during communism, we went to a pierogi kiosk at the beach and the clerk said, 'I'm sorry, the cook didn't have time to make any today.' "

I said, "I was in Estonia during commie times looking for a restaurant, but they were all closed and displayed signs in the windows that said, *Accident.* I went back later, and they had changed the signs to say, *Closed so that the staff can have dinner.*"

Ludmila looked uncomfortable, so I stopped talking. She had probably benefitted from communism since only performers who espoused orthodox views would have been allowed on television.

Wojtek spoke next. "They also displayed signs that said, *Restaurant Full.* The doors were locked and they would only let someone in from the queue outside if someone came out. If you looked through the window, the restaurant was mostly empty. The staff were sitting with their elbows on the tables, propping their sagging heads up on their hands, looking terribly bored."

Jadwiga said, "This was our Russian-communist, workers' paradise," and then returned to whispering confidences with Jack. They kissed tenderly each time they were interrupted by the sound of clinking glasses. Uncles and aunts with sweat-stained armpits gave glowing speeches about Jadwiga's accomplishments. Wojtek proposed a toast to their father, and Ludmila wiped a tear.

When it came my turn to give a speech, I congratulated the bride and groom and talked about Australia and the strong, upstanding, heroic men it produces. In order not to draw attention to Jack's lack of representation, I consciously avoided saying that I had only known him for a short time.

"What happens after the dinner?" I asked Katya after returning to my seat.

"Accordions and polkas, and more eating."

"Oczepiny ceremony." Jadwiga's mother did understand English after all.

"You know English!" I exclaimed and she squirmed.

"Nowadays, oczepiny ceremony looks totally different," Jadwiga's sister Diana explained. "It is funny midnight games when a groom with his best men try to get the bride's veil. A group of unmarried maidens make a circle around the bride to protect her from the groom. After a few moments, the veil is taken from the bride's head and she throws it to the maidens. The one who catches it will get married first."

Jadwiga and Jack danced the first dance together, which was a waltz. This was followed by a polka and as many as could fit on the floor joined in. I escorted Katya to the perimeter and danced her over to the bridal couple.

"You're doing all right," I said. "Did you learn to dance like that in Australia?"

Jack had to stop dancing to answer. "We got some lessons from a gay dance-instructor second cousin. He had to take the female part to show me. When I apologized to him for the awkwardness, he said, 'No worries. I am a *dance instructor*,' like this was a sacred vocation."

"*It is*," Jadwiga said. She wasn't as good as Hana, but she really liked dancing.

Diana appropriated Jack and spun him around the floor enthu-siastically, her buxomness barely restrained by her corset top. The three-piece band was composed of electric guitar, drums and accordion. They struck up a seriously hard-rocking version of *White Wedding* with the accordion player belting out the gravel-throated, Billy-Idol vocals.

After Jadwiga tossed her veil, Wojtek marshalled Jack into the centre of the room, shook his hand and instructed him to fling his bow tie over his shoulder. The soon-to-be-wed girl who had caught the veil boldly walked over to dance with the man who caught the tie. The older men stood watching from the sidelines at a table where aromatic sausage links were hanging as in a butcher shop.

The evening continued with people dancing around hand-kerchiefs, fortune tellers in Romani costumes, games of musical chairs and the shoe game. Husbands and wives were invited to answer questions about each other by holding up the shoe of the spouse who was most likely to fit a description or behaviour.

One other interesting thing happened. At around midnight, it was Jadwiga's and Jack's turn at the shoe game. They had picked each other's shoes in response to the question, *Which of you is the more romantic?* I noticed a drunk, young man stagger through the doorway to the hall and stand watching from a corner. His clothes and hair looked dishevelled.

He wailed, "Tak bardzo cie kocham," which temporarily stopped the proceedings. A group of uncles surrounded him and gently eased him back out the door. His arms flailed in a half-hearted attempt at resistance.

"What was that?" I asked Katya.

"I don't know. He said, 'I love you so much,' in Polish. I guess he really likes weddings."

We got back to our hotel around 3 a.m. with an invitation to reconvene for lunch. Katya came into the bathroom to brush her teeth. "How's your wasp bite. It doesn't look like it's getting any better."

"It doesn't itch like a normal bug bite. It's been hurting. Take another picture for me." I handed my phone to her.

She aimed carefully and handed me back the phone. I pinched the image wide to scrutinize it. The picture showed that the welt had grown to about three centimetres in diameter. It was raised and angry-looking with a central punctum. "It looks worse, doesn't it? It's probably all the dancing and sweating."

"Maybe you should go to the emergency department and have it checked." There was concern in her voice.

"That costs money here. I don't react well to wasp bites. It might also be getting infected. Polish doctors wouldn't be able to tell me anything I can't figure out for myself. I'm not febrile." I felt the front of my neck and underarms. "I don't have any swollen lymph nodes. I'll start taking some antibiotics to be safe. I have a supply of out-dated Keflex in my suitcase that I've been carrying around for years."

"Jadwiga could look at it for you."

"I don't think she could tell me anything either."

Chapter 23

W e slept for six hours and then dragged our sorry asses to Ludmila's apartment to attend the proprawiny, or after-party. I was carrying my rumpled rental tux and shiny plastic shoes in a garment bag for Agnies to return. I'd eaten so much meat in Poland that my shit had turned black, the colour of shit in alcoholics with gastrointestinal bleeding.

The leftover food and suspended sausage links had been trans-ported here intact. The uncles may have been wearing the same clothes as the previous evening. The sausages, which they were gathered around and sampling reverentially, seemed to have a magnetic attraction.

"Do you think they've been to bed?" I asked Katya.

"Some of them definitely not. I'm going to go speak Polish with Ludmila."

I approached the uncles, most of whom I had not had the chance to chat with yet. They looked to be in their fifties and sixties and were redolent of garlic and metabolized alcohol. They greeted me like a long-lost brother. One of them was in the middle of telling a joke in Polish, which he started again from the beginning in English for my benefit.

"A man goes to a police station in Russia to report his parrot missing. 'What's so special about this bird?' the policeman asks. 'It talks a lot. I came to report that I don't agree with its opinions.' "

The joke was met with uproarious laughter. These were the same uncles who had escorted the unruly drunk out the door last night. "You must be the marriage police. I noticed you keeping order at the party last night."

"Yes, we are," the joke teller said and slapped my back hard.

Another uncle slurred, "Putin gives a speech on TV. He says that thanks to reforms he introduced, people are now allowed to get rich. Here is the list of people." Everyone laughed again, but I had the feeling that they had heard the joke before. "Matthias, you are Canadian, yes? Are these jokes funny in Canada? Do people know about Putin?"

"Absolutely. Everyone would laugh in Canada." I said, although it probably wasn't true.

"Do you have such jokes about your Prime Minister Trudeau?"

I racked my brains to think of one about Justin Trudeau but came up empty. "We mostly tell jokes about American leaders," I said.

"Of course, it is normal. We both sleep beside elephants." He cut a thick slice from one of the links of sausage and offered it to me. I tasted animal fat, smoke, salt and nitrites. Yum.

I asked the group: "Do you think that the West should have been a more generous winner in 1991 and poured money into Russia at the end of the Cold War, the way they did with the Marshall Plan in Germany after World War II? Should they have invited Russia into the EU and NATO as they did with Poland? We might have had a different world order."

The uncles looked at each other and the one with the clearest head and best English answered. "Matthias, if you invested $100 in Germany at the end of the war, you got $100 worth of renovation. If you invested $100 in Russia, it would all get stolen."

Every man in the group shook my hand. They resumed speaking in hungover Polish and I wandered back to Katya. "They were quoting

Pierre Elliott Trudeau to me about when you sleep beside an elephant, you are affected by its every twitch."

"I have more information about the drunk guy who screamed, 'I love you,' at the party last night," Katya said. "That was Jadwiga's ex-fiancé."

"No kidding? Wow. I wasn't watching her. How did she react?"

"She was smiling, but she looked sad. She looked down the whole time. He was at the wedding too—standing all alone at the back of the church."

"I didn't notice. He's *married* now, isn't he?"

"Yes. He's still married. He had contacted Jadwiga to tell her that he regretted his choice. One of the reasons Jadwiga went to America was to avoid him and to get her emotions back on an even keel. Ludmila said that he also screamed, 'Love means you never have to say you're sorry,' in Polish."

"Again, wow. It's a good thing that they're moving far away from him. Ludmila looks well put together but not all-out happy."

"She doesn't want Jadwiga to move to Australia. It's too far to visit."

"Was your mother pleased with your match?"

"Doctor was her first choice," Katya said. "Businessman was second."

"Ah, yes. Businessman has a magical ring."

Jadwiga waved and approached from across the room. "Did you get some tea, Matthias?" Tea meant lunch, dinner or the beverage in Australian English.

"Yes, super good and tasty. That was a beautiful wedding, Jadwiga—possibly the most beautiful wedding ever, and you are tied with Katya for the most beautiful bride ever."

"Thank you, Matthias. Katya told me that you have a sore neck. May I see your neck please?"

"It's the day after the day of your wedding. You're still off duty today, Jadwiga."

"No worries, mate. May I see your neck please?"

"Show her your neck, hon. Don't make her beg," Katya said.

I undid my top two shirt buttons and pulled the shirt down off my shoulder.

"There is a hole in your neck. How did you get this, Matthias? Maybe we should go to the hospital for an X-ray. I have a friend who works there in the X-ray department."

"My spine's not broken. X-rays show bones, not inflamed soft tissue, Jadwiga." My tone sounded superior, like Canadian doctors are better than Polish doctors, which they are.

"Of course, Matthias. You know best."

"I'm sorry, Jadwiga. I react badly to wasp bites. I started taking an antibiotic that I brought with me. We'll be back in Canada tomorrow evening. I'll get it checked out as soon as I get home."

"Please do so, Matthias."

"Are you honeymooning in beautiful Polska, Jadwiga?" Katya asked.

"Niagara Falls is the honeymoon capital of the world," I reminded her.

"Yes. We are travelling with the Interrail Pass to many tourist spots, but first we have, for one night, a special room in the Grand Hotel Sopot."

"We were just there. Did we give you the idea?" I asked.

"Yes. It was your very good idea, Matthias."

"Don't go into the casino. They specialize in separating newly-weds from their money."

"No, Matthias. We will not go there unless we get a very good tip from a fortune teller with a kind face." She had crinkles at the corners of her eyes that would some day be etched there for Jack to love.

185

"Will I see you again before we leave tomorrow?" I asked. "If not, I'll kiss the bride now."

"Matthias, you are of course welcome to kiss the bride now, but I am staying in the same hotel as you and coming to the airport with you tomorrow."

"In that case, I'll wait until tomorrow so you don't think I'm a lecher."

Jadwiga pulled out her phone to look up the word. When she got the meaning, she gave me a hug anyway and then gave one to Katya.

I was erring on the side of caution. Katya had told me that my godfather, who is now deceased, had tried to slip her the tongue whenever they greeted. I had always thought he was a gentleman. My sister told me that he had done the same to my mother.

Katya and I spent the evening in our hotel room packing. I asked her whether Jack knew about Jadwiga's ex-fiancé being at the wedding. She said she didn't think so and I shouldn't tell him. Katya was afraid that I might spook him. He was happy. Why complicate things? Men don't really want to know about their wives' past love lives. I couldn't agree more.

We gathered in the hotel restaurant in the morning for breakfast. Wojtek arrived to join us and to give us a lift to the airport.

"Well, this is it," I said. "Our last historic breakfast. We have to say goodbye to all this history and culture."

"I think you like history also, Matthias," Jadwiga said. "You are becoming more Polish."

Robert studied history to avoid repeating mistakes of the past. I said, "Knowing the history of my parents and grandparents' lives makes me feel like I've lived a longer life than I'll ever be able. It's interesting to know the series of accidents that led to my existence. If Germany hadn't attacked Russia in World War II, my parents would never have met."

"If the Treaty of Versailles that ended the First World War had treated Germany less severely, Hitler wouldn't have come to power," Wojtek said. "If Archduke Franz Ferdinand had not been assassinated, there would have been no First World War. Would you like me to keep going?"

"Where would you be if you didn't exist, Matthias?" Jadwiga asked.

"Nowhere probably."

"Do you think that you are also an accident, Jack?" Jadwiga asked.

I held my breath because I considered accident a taboo word for him.

Jack paused and said, "Humanity is an accident on a cosmic scale. Without the meteor that struck the earth extinguishing the dinosaurs, the largest, meanest, meat-eating reptiles would have continued to dominate. The majority of planets on which life has developed would not have experienced a mass extinction event like ours to get rid of their brutes."

I was impressed. Wojtek said, "That is quite an insight, but we still have plenty of brutes."

"The past is history, the future is a mystery, the present is a gift," Jack said. "I think we should head for Paris, the city of light, and make stops all along the way. What do you reckon, Jadwiga?"

Jadwiga responded by reaching over to give Jack an embrace that lasted five seconds.

"Paris is for lovers," Katya said.

Wojtek thought that five people plus luggage wouldn't fit in his small car. We hugged it out with Jadwiga and Jack, with three cheek kisses each—two on one cheek and one on the other, like French people.

"I owe you and Katya, maybe my life," Jack told me.

"The best things that happen are the things that you don't plan. I wish you every happiness. I'm sorry your train trip across Canada was so murdery."

"Are you coming for the repeat performance in Australia?"

"Send me an invite anyway. Are you going to be a dentist again when you get home?"

"I have a non-compete agreement with the corporation I sold my surgery to. It will have to be in a different Australian city."

"Are dentists generally in demand in Australia?"

"The good thing about being a dentist is that teeth only deteriorate. Teeth rot your entire life, and when they're gone, you'll need implants or a pair of clackers. After you're dead, they last forever."

I was walking beside Wojtek as were carrying our luggage through the parking lot. I asked him, "Would you ever consider moving away from Poland?"

"Never, old bean. If everyone did that, who would be left to defend it?"

His mother would be glad to hear that. Wojtek drove us to Gdansk Lech Walesa airport. It turned out that five would fit in his car. It was a cramped ride with conversation shouted over the sound of the muffler. In contrast to Wojtek's patriotism, Jadwiga's parting words were a jubilant invitation to come and spend next Christmas on the beach with them in Australia. With a connection in Warsaw, we would be in Toronto by 9 p.m.

There were two cardiac surgeons on the trans-Atlantic flight. I heard the announcement for any doctors or other medical personnel to please come to the front of the plane to deal with a medical emergency. As I was arriving, I met one walking toward me. He introduced himself and told me that I wasn't needed. He didn't tell me why not. I am not used to having my credentials trumped. I met the second one coming forward as I was walking back to my seat. He must have counted to 20 before getting up to help.

Chapter 24

Ontario, Canada

My son Michael's apartment was on the way home from the airport. Although it was late, we had to stop by to pick up our dog. We detoured off the highway and texted him when we were parked outside.

Michael came out to meet us and invited us in. We declined because Harper had to work in the morning and was already asleep. The dog's celebratory barking would have woken her. We gave him a medium and a large babushka-hand-knit sweater souvenir in exchange for the dog, her basket and her kibble.

"You're wearing your old glasses," he said. "I thought you lost them in Banff."

"I found them in Gdansk, Poland. The circumstances are a little worrying. They reappeared on a night table in my hotel room."

"Are you sure they weren't in your suitcase the whole time? Maybe the room cleaner saw them and put them on the table for you."

"I don't think so."

Michael had degrees in computer science and software engineering and was my reference for technology questions. When he was a child, he used to say that he knew everything but he just couldn't do everything. He still did seem to know everything.

"Do you think it matters that I used hotel Wi-Fi in Poland to access the coroners' encrypted website in Canada?" It had seemed urgent to know Hana Sato's toxicology report at the time that I accessed it in Poland. I could have waited.

"Not really. Not if it was encrypted. Wi-Fi is generally encrypted now."

"Would it have been better to use my cell phone?"

"Not really. Are we talking about Russians again? You said a Russian woman stole your glasses. If we're talking about nation-states, the Edward Snowden revelations show that there's nothing they can't do. They can exfiltrate data from offline computers by inducing them to broadcast sound waves and then measuring slight vibrations of windows with lasers. Cell phone towers are no more secure than hotel Wi-Fi."

"Would I have revealed my cellphone number or any personal information on my phone by using public Wi-Fi?"

"Yes and no. That information is usually online somewhere already. Almost everyone's personal information has been compromised by data breaches at companies they have dealt with online. You flew TAP, the Portuguese airline, a few years ago. You stayed at the MGM Grand Hotel in Las Vegas."

"When are you and Harper coming to visit?" Katya interrupted. This reminded me of the times we had visited Katya's parents' house when they were alive. Her mother would follow us out to the street, nearly hugging our ankles, asking the same question, and we would give a non-committal answer.

"Not the next couple of weekends. Harper has made plans to visit friends and we're going to a concert in Toronto the first weekend of next month."

"Okay, but soon," Katya said.

We settled Madame Fifi in her basket on the back seat and Katya gave Michael a farewell hug standing in the street.

I exchanged fist bumps with Michael, and then a hug. He might have thought I was showing signs of early dementia. I preferred that to worrying him with my suspicions.

I still had a day off before returning to work in the O.R. It was reserved for unpacking and going through my backlog of mail after a good night's sleep. A lot of my emails were notifications and policy updates for coroners, which I browsed and filed. I went onto the coroners' website to enter the information about Hana Sato's negative toxicology into her case history.

This prompted me to go onto the Coventry Hospital website to check if John Hartley's cholinesterase level was back. A low level would be evidence of organophosphorus poisoning, since these poisons are cholinesterase inhibitors. The test had to be sent out because our lab didn't do it. It still wasn't back.

There was lingering inflammation in my neck, but it wasn't getting any worse. I telephoned Jason McMurray, my family doctor, and was able to get an appointment for the same afternoon. This was of course due to my insider status. I cycled ten minutes to his office building to avoid the mandatory usurious parking fee.

After Jason examined me, he said, "If it's not healing, perhaps we should get an X-ray."

"What would that show?" I asked.

"Let's find out."

It was extremely difficult to find family doctors, so I didn't argue with him and pedalled off to the hospital for an X-ray. Two days later, I got a phone call from Jason.

"There's a round metallic foreign body in your neck. Did you get shot with a pellet gun while you were in Poland?"

"I don't know." It dawned on me that that was what must have happened.

"Do you want me to refer you to anyone to have it taken out?" Jason asked.

"If they can do it under local. I'm not having a general anesthetic."

"You can dish the anesthetics out, but you can't take them, eh? That's not a very good recommendation."

"I would only accept a general anesthetic if the condition that I had was life threatening. I know what can go wrong."

"You would probably need a light general. The pellet is at a depth of two centimetres. It might settle down on antibiotics. Metal is usually pretty inert. Why don't we check it again in a week."

Before doing anything else, I texted Thomas: *I was shot in the neck with a pellet in Poland. Could we meet to talk this over?* He asked for a list of days that I was available. We arranged to meet for lunch at a brewpub in Elora on my day off after my next night on call. It was roughly halfway between Coventry and Toronto.

Surgeons say that there is no minor surgery, only minor surgeons. The same applies to anesthetics. A "light general anesthetic" still took away your airway reflexes and rendered you susceptible to complications such as airway trauma, laryngospasm, allergic reactions, aspiration of gastric contents, etcetera.

I had access to surgeons with whom I worked, but I didn't mention it to any of them. I've seen extremely frustrated surgeons rooting around for foreign bodies. After an hour they say, "It really should be right there, and let's just extend the incision a little." Of course, a metallic foreign body would be visible on portable X-ray, but if the foreign body is glass or a wood splinter, they may never find it.

Researching BB gun pellets online, I discovered that they were historically made of lead. The newer ones were steel. Steel pellets were approximately four millimeters in diameter, while the lead ones were approximately five.

After finishing an operating list, I wandered down to the radiology department and asked to see Liam, a radiologist with whom I was friendly. I found him peering at a large illuminated screen in a small dark room, dictating into a microphone. He stopped talking when he noticed me lingering in the doorway.

We exchanged greetings, and I asked him to pull up my X-ray and have a look at it with me. As Jason, my family doctor, had reported, the X-ray showed a solid white circle in the soft tissue between my shoulder and spine.

Liam said, "Lead and steel are equally radio-opaque." He held a clear plastic ruler over the image of the projectile. "There would be no way to distinguish on the basis of a one-millimetre diameter difference. Projection artifact could easily be one millimetre. It's not completely radio-opaque. There are some striations or filaments. Are you going to have it out?"

"I don't know yet. It might be okay to leave it."

He resumed dictating in the dark and I closed the door behind him. Reading X-rays looked like a job that A.I. would be doing in the near future. A few humans could supervise quality control during the transition phase.

It used to be thought that you could safely leave lead bullets in place in the human body. That thinking is changing. It's controversial now because leaving them has actually led to lead poisoning. It generally takes years for that to happen. The symptoms are memory loss, mood disorders and fatigue.

I have these symptoms already, but I have had them for a while. I can't remember how long. They are probably the result of hockey and car accident-related concussions. The current standard of care still is to leave lead bullets in place until you see the symptoms developing.

Lead arsenic alloys are for sale on the internet for industrial use. What if the pellet was an alloy of lead and arsenic? What if it was some other poisonous heavy metal like cadmium or mercury? They are all available online. Since they are metals, they all look the same on X-ray.

I telephoned Jason to ask if I could get a blood lead level to help me decide on whether to have the pellet surgically removed. He agreed but said that he doubted that the test would be useful.

"Okay. Do I have to pay for that?" I asked.

"I wouldn't think so. They used to test lead levels on kids years ago pretty routinely. I'll put down that you have occupational exposure."

"In a way, that's true." I was thinking, if get shot in pursuance of my coronial duties. I stopped short of asking him for a full battery of heavy-metal screening tests. He might refuse and in future regard me as just another paranoid hypochondriac.

At the appointed time for our rendezvous in Elora, Thomas was waiting for me at a window table and waved me over. "Hey Matt! Good to see you. I've been wanting to try this restaurant. A buddy of mine recommended it. Check out the view."

"Nice." The Elora River and Gorge were visible. "It's not exactly private."

"We're not going to say anything secret. Order what you want. We're on an expense account today."

"Okay, thanks." I sat down across the table from him. "Where are you based?"

"I'm based in Toronto. So, you were shot in the neck in Poland with a BB gun and you suspect Russians."

"Yes. My glasses that were stolen from me in the Banff Springs Hotel turned up on my night table in Gdansk, Poland."

"Right. You said that. Okay, it's probably Russians."

"So, now what. Do I need protection?"

"I would say not. The typical Russian manners of death are poisoning and defenestration—being thrown out of a window. That's from time immemorial," Thomas said. "They also occasionally like downing aircraft. I don't think they would kill a planeload of people just to get one guy, unless everyone on board was a target like the Wagner group."

"Like Prigozhin."

"They *would* probably poison a guy on a plane though because there would be no medical assistance until the plane lands and, even after that, it would be delayed."

"Like Navalny."

"Yes, poor sap. Putin was always going to kill him, but he's gone on a real killing spree since invading Ukraine. He's all in."

"The airlines rely on random doctors and nurses who might be on board their planes," I said. "They would be pretty useless without diagnostic labs and poison antidotes. They would probably diagnose Novichok poisoning as gastroenteritis…" Like I did with Anastasia on the flight from Calgary to Toronto. I had forgotten to ask whether she was an enemy of the Russian state.

"They give you a slow death with polonium if they want you to suffer and they want to send a message," Thomas said. "Polonium-210 is radioactive, but it's undetectable carrying it through border crossings or airports. It only emits alpha particles, not gamma rays. Alpha particles are shielded by anything as flimsy as a piece of paper. It's still lethal after a few weeks if you ingest it."

"Could they shoot it from a pellet gun?"

"I guess so. I've never heard of that. Markov, the Bulgarian writer, was assassinated in London in the 1970s by a ricin pellet shot into his leg from the tip of an umbrella. He was dead four days later. You seem to have made it home from Poland all right."

"Yes, I'm still here."

"How long has it been since you were shot?"

"Two weeks."

"It's intimidation to let you know you're vulnerable. Check out the menu. I'm thinking of having the kimchi burger with spicy mayo."

"So, do nothing?" I asked.

"Don't piss off any more Russians and you should be fine. It was just a warning, like waving away a fly that's buzzing close to your ear. You wouldn't make the effort to kill it unless it came inside your house."

I glanced at the menu. "There was a woman on the flight to Poland sitting next to me who turned up again in Gdansk where I was staying. Maybe she shot me."

"Don't you believe in coincidences?"

"No. After he retired from the Toronto Police, my father worked for Radio Liberty in Washington and Munich, broadcasting American propaganda to the godless commies. Would they hold that against me?"

"Maybe, but probably not. *Although*, one of our Moscow embassy staff was murdered in Russia for being gay. Look, if you have the pellet surgically removed, send it to me and I'll get it analyzed."

"Really? Our lab at the Centre for Forensic Sciences will only analyze body fluids—nothing solid like a pellet. Of course, they wouldn't do me anyway since I'm not dead yet."

"Careful what you wish for. I do have some other news for you though, Matt. Congratulations are in order," he said enthusiastically.

"Why? Did you find the two Russians from the train?"

"No, not that. As the coroner for the Japanese national, Hana Sato, you'll be interested to know that Novichok was confirmed in post-mortem blood samples and on the toothbrushes from the train. Our American friends did the analysis."

It took a moment to process the information. "I'm glad I didn't touch the toothbrushes. John Hartley's body mass was twice hers. That's why he wasn't killed outright."

"That sounds right," Thomas said. "The assassins wouldn't have known which toothbrush was his, so they poisoned them both. Hush now. The waiter's coming. What do you want to eat?"

My neck felt sore. "The kimchi burger sounds good, and a no-alcohol beer."

After the waiter left, I asked, "Why do you think there were two assassins on the train? Do they need backup assassins? Wouldn't that draw attention?"

"Novichok is a binary agent. Each guy carries one inactive ingredient. They combined them on the train. It's too dangerous to carry mixed. Just a drop on your skin could kill you. Like I said, send me the pellet if you haven't suddenly dropped dead." He smiled to show me he was joking.

"Is this going to be released to the press?"

"My impression is that in the wake of Covid, the wars in Ukraine and Gaza, global warming, illegal immigration and the U.S. election, the politicians don't want more public hysteria. Bon appetit."

Hana Sato and John Hartley—that made two homicides in Coventry. I'd only had one probable homicide case before in my ten-year career as a coroner. The evidence for that one wasn't conclusive, and Richard Tull had told me to record the manner of death as undetermined. The victim was an excommunicated, drug-dealing Mennonite. That doesn't happen very often.

Chapter 25

My family doctor telephoned me a week later. "How are you feeling, Matt?"

"Good thanks. What's new?"

"I got your lead level back. I thought you might be interested."

"Yes. What was it?"

"Three micrograms per decilitre. That level isn't dangerous, but the normal level is zero. Do you eat a lot of shellfish?"

"Only occasionally. My father did tell me to syphon leaded gas out of his car's tank to fuel our lawn mower when I was a kid. I remember swallowing some by accident."

"How often did you do that?"

"A few times."

"That could be it. Lead stays in your body forever, in your bones. Did you get that pellet taken out of your neck?"

"No, not yet."

"Well, it's up to you. You might want to think about it."

"Thanks. I will."

"Good. I suggest we repeat the test in a few months."

Not wanting insidious progression of my symptoms to the point where I would be too demented to recognize them, I checked the operating room schedule to see when Chandler Davis was working next.

Chandler was a young general surgeon in Coventry who had impressed me with his skill. He didn't have a huge ego yet, so we were on friendly terms. I cornered him in his operating room one day between cases and explained the situation. He pulled up my X-ray on the viewing box in the room to see the location of the pellet.

"That should be pretty easy," he said. "It's radio-opaque, so it will show up on the C-Arm X-ray. It looks like it's embedded in the trapezius muscle, not near anything vital."

"Do you think you could do it under local anesthetic?"

"We could try it that way first. If we do it that way, it would be best to have an anesthesiologist present to give you some sedation. Are you uncomfortable with a general anesthetic?"

"Yes."

"Okay. Let's plan to do it under local with IV sedation. I'll ask my secretary to call you with an appointment date."

"Can you keep the pellet for me? I have a colleague who will check its composition."

"Why? It's not radio-active, is it?"

"I hope not. Someone shot me in a random, incognito act of violence." I didn't feel like explaining the circumstances further.

It was very possible that part way through the procedure, if the surgeon was having trouble, he would ask for a general anesthetic. Anesthetic complications during elective surgery were extremely rare with all of our anesthesiologists. Nevertheless, I wasn't content to let just anyone on staff be in charge of keeping me alive.

Chandler's secretary called to tell me that my surgery would be tacked onto the end of his operating room list in a week. Making a switch of anesthesiologist in a published O.R. list was sure to give offence to someone, so I looked through the schedule in advance to see who was working that day. Of the listed anesthesiologists, Zack White was my favourite.

I texted Zach to ask that he choose my room. Being asked by a colleague was sort of an honour because it advertised that he was the élite choice, but also an imposition, because he might have to forego a more lucrative list to accommodate me. If one survived undamaged, an expensive bottle of wine was the customary token compensation.

On the day of my surgery, I told Katya not to bother coming with me because I was having a local anesthetic. I parked in the doctors' parking lot and checked in at the front desk of the operating room. The clerk diffidently took my information to register me.

Sara came to the desk to lead me to the staging area. "Hi Matt. I'm the circulating nurse in your room today. Are you here for a prostatectomy or a penile implant?"

"I'll probably need both at some point, but it's not a urological problem. I've just got a foreign body here." I pointed to my neck.

"Robert, the medical student on urology was looking for you."

"What for?"

"He didn't say actually. What have you got in your neck?"

"Someone shot me when I was visiting Poland."

"What? Why? You don't know who?"

"No. I suspect Russians."

"It's not safe anywhere anymore, is it. Okay, please change into a hospital gown, open at the back. You know the drill, Matt. You have to park your dignity. I'll leave the intravenous up to the anesthesiologist. I don't want you getting angry with me if I miss."

"I wouldn't be angry, just disappointed, Sara."

"No thanks," she said.

Big tall Robert in O.R. greens appeared at my bedside. "Hi Dr. Kork. I'm in the room with you today."

"I thought you were a urology resident now."

"The boss has the day off today, so I'm back to being an anesthesiologist. Can I start your IV for you?"

Thinking that I would give him exactly one chance, I held out my left arm. I felt Robert tighten a rubber tourniquet around my upper arm, wipe the skin of my hand and insert the needle. I didn't watch because that increases the pain of the needle stick—by exactly twice as much if my watching Robert made him nervous enough to miss.

"Someone's taught you well," I said when I saw that he had been successful. He was more competent than I was at his stage. Sara handed him the intravenous tubing and applied a sterile dressing after it was connected.

"Thanks chief," Robert said. "How's Jadwiga doing? Is she still staying with you?"

"No, she's gone back to Poland. Out of sight, out of mind."

"I called her up for a second date, but she said she couldn't make it."

"Who's Jadwiga?" Sara asked.

"Dr. Kork's wife's niece. I think I'll text her later after work."

"I heard she got married, Robert."

"Oh yeah? Who'd she marry?"

"I heard it was a guy who needed her more than you," I said.

"Plenty of fish in the sea, Robert," Sara said. She wasn't ruling herself out.

Zach arrived, reviewed my chart and pushed my stretcher into the operating room. Sara and Robert were hanging onto the sides of the stretcher like I was a prize catch. I moved myself onto the operating table, positioned myself on my side and submitted to the application of monitors and an oxygen mask.

I said, "Robert, if you don't mind, I'd prefer to have Zach administer the anesthetic if I end up needing one. I mean not delegating any aspect of it."

"Yes sir."

"Don't give me any sedation unless I ask for it, please, Zach," I said. "I'm pretty tough."

Chandler entered the room, said hello to everyone, and scrubbed and draped my neck. Sara put a lead gown over my gonads. I felt the burn of the local anesthetic as Chandler injected it under my skin. There was more burning as Chandler cut the skin and then just dull tugging. The C-arm X-ray machine loomed over my head.

After half an hour had passed when no one spoke, Chandler said, "I think I need him asleep."

I heard my heart rate rising and the alarm on the blood pressure monitor indicating that it had gone over a pre-set upper limit. "I'm fine," I insisted from under the drapes. "You can keep going as long as you like."

"Well, okay then. I'll give it a little longer," Chandler said, sounding dubious.

Zach said, "I'm going to give you some sedation, Matt." I felt myself fading and then pass into oblivion.

My next recollection was being in the recovery room with a fat lip, surrounded by monitors and other patients in bed bays surrounded by more monitors. I had experienced the death and resurrection that I meted out daily.

"Here it is," Chandler said, He was standing at my bedside, shaking a translucent plastic specimen jar with something rattling inside. "I'm going to leave it with you on your bedside table."

"Thanks," I slurred. "Did it take long to find?"

"I got it right after you went to sleep. You were only out for a minute or two. It was right there the whole time. It's bigger than I thought and kind of capsule shaped. The X-ray must have caught it end-on to make it look round."

A few minutes later, Robert came to check up on me. "How are you feeling, Dr. Kork? We got that pellet out of your neck for you."

"I'm fine thanks, Robert. Just a bit of a fat lip. Did you have to use an airway while I was asleep?"

"Not me, chief. Dr. White put a laryngeal mask airway in your mouth. It was a little awkward because you were on your side."

"It must have dragged my lip over my teeth when he put it in."

"When you were waking up, you yanked it out of your mouth, said, 'What the fuck is this?' and threw it across the room."

"I did that? You'd think I'd know what a vagina looked like. Pulling it out wouldn't have given me a fat lip."

"Should have let me insert it, Dr. Kork. I would have been more careful." Robert was a *can-do* guy.

After an hour, I pulled myself together and got my clothes on. With the pellet in the plastic jar rattling in my pocket, a hard-working, little female porter put me in a wheelchair and wheeled me down the corridor to the elevator. I was twice her size and pretty much awake.

Once inside the elevator, I said, "Okay let's change places, Carol. You deserve a free ride more than I do."

"Are you sure? I might get fired if someone sees us."

"Okay. I wouldn't want you to get fired."

Her pushing me the rest of the way to the front door must have looked ridiculous. Once there, I jumped up, thanked her, grabbed a waiting cab and went home. Katya was in the kitchen emptying the dishwasher.

"How was your procedure? Did they get the pellet out?" she asked.

"Yes." I held up the bottle with the pellet. "I had to have a general. I took a cab home. Robert says hello."

She looked at the bottle, at the bandage on my neck and said, "I'm glad that's over with. Is it sore?"

"No. I'm glad you like emptying the dishwasher. I find it tedious."

"I don't like doing it."

"Oh, I thought you did. We have fewer dishes again, now that Jadwiga and Jack are gone, but it's still fills up. You told me that you liked doing it."

"I don't like it," Katya said. "I was lying cause I love you, hon."

"Maybe cause it's every goddamned day."

"Yes. I love you every goddamned day."

Katya drove me back to work at the hospital the next morning. I had a list of total joint replacements in the orthopedic room. I have a pair of earplugs that I use during orthopedic surgery to dampen the sound of the metal-on-metal hammering. When the hammering was done for the day, I wrapped the pellet in some gauze, and put it in the small plastic case for the earplugs.

My vehicle was waiting for me in the doctors' lot. I drove it to the post office where they sold me a padded envelope, which I used to mail the pellet to the address on Thomas' business card.

Zappa was in the corner of the Rec Centre weight room when I arrived. He was stacking large metal plates onto both ends of a bar that was beginning to bow in the middle. His back and shoulders were bulging out of his sleeveless wife-beater T-shirt. The limp was gone. I went over to ask about his health.

"Hi Zappa. You don't seem to need your cane anymore."

"No. I got rid of that after a week. My leg is mostly better now."

"I always suspected that exercise was the cure for everything. A doctor's job is to entertain you while you get better on your own."

"They don't know everything. I have to work out every day. I'm an addict. Where's your Aussie buddy?"

"He got married in Poland recently. He's on his honeymoon. I was the best man at his wedding."

"He was kicking that heavy bag like a trained killer. Did you give him a good bachelor party send-off?"

"No. It was very sudden. They only decided when they were visiting her family in Poland. He used to say that a woman's breasts were shaped like tears."

"That's a very bad attitude," Zappa said. "Did you have anything to do with changing his mind?"

"I think you did, Zappa, more than me."

"Is he coming back here? I could help you out with that bachelor party."

"Well, he's already married now."

"Mandy!" Zappa called. "Come on over and say hello."

Mandy, who was wearing sweat pants and a halter top, stopped doing latissimus pull-downs a few machines away and came over.

"Amanda, meet Matt—Dr. Kork."

"You're looking good, Mandy," I said, "like you've been working out a lot."

"Thanks." Mandy looked me over appraisingly.

"That's Mandy's livelihood," Zappa said. "Amanda, how would you and one or two of the girls feel about doing your act at a bachelor party?"

"Good. Three hundred bucks each for an hour. No happy endings."

"Of course not, Mandy." Zappa winked. "Matt, you good with that?"

"Can they do the show in Australia?" I asked.

"How far is that?" Mandy asked.

"No, that's probably too far," Zappa said, "but I meant when he comes back here. The guy is actually already married, Mandy, but he missed his party."

"Sure, no problem. Married but not buried," Amanda said. "Are you a real doctor, or just like a DJ?"

"He's a real doctor but not the kind of doctor you would ever want to visit. Thanks Mandy."

"I could probably do it for $250," Mandy said.

"We'll let you know, Mandy," Zappa said.

"Did they have a buck n' doe?"

"They didn't have one of those either," I said.

"You can make a lot of money on those." Mandy went back to her workout.

"Does that sound all right?" Zappa asked. "I probably shouldn't have told her you were a doctor. She jacked the price up a bit. When's your friend coming back?"

"He hasn't told me. He texted me that he was opening a new dental office in Brisbane, Australia. I'm only sorry we didn't think of doing this before he went to Europe."

"Of course, some of the other girls are full service."

"I wouldn't be looking for that," I said.

"Need any workout stuff? Did I tell you I got a website? All the newest stuff is on there."

"You carry the convict-stripe design for Australians?"

"For anybody."

"I like the colours I've seen you wearing. I don't think the wife-beater T-shirt is a good look for me."

"I would never use it for that purpose." Zappa said in a matter-of-fact tone. He added more 20-kilogram plates to his bar and went back to massive muscle maintenance.

A couple of days after my surgery, I received an anonymous text: *In future, let's not quibble about who killed whom.* I considered replying, *Fuck you,* or *Suck a dick,* or something equally witty, but settled on not acknowledging or engaging and blocking the number.

Chapter 26

Thomas called me.

"Is there something you're not telling me about yourself, Matthew?"

"No. What do you mean?"

"It was a tracking device."

"What was?"

"In your shoulder. It was a device that used your cell phone as a beacon to transmit your location. Any cell phone near you would also do it."

"Not poison?"

"No. Like a miniature electronic luggage tag."

"They can make a battery that small?"

"You were the battery. They must have been trying to find out who you are. You were with Hammersmith in Vancouver, with Max von Scheffel in Banff. You turned up to investigate Hana Sato's death, turned up again at the hospital when the guy was being treated for bear spray in his eyes, then again in Toronto to identify his partner, again at Hammersmith's killing and then in Poland."

"Those were all coincidences."

"I thought you didn't believe in coincidences."

"What's wrong with being in Poland?" I asked.

"Jadwiga Bilecki. Her father was Polish military intelligence, until his untimely death."

"He died in a car crash. He was a drunk or he suicided."

"No. Listen—your habit of coincidentally turning up every-where has attracted attention. I have a proposition for you."

"Why did they have to shoot me? They could have just em-bedded the transmitter in the frame of my glasses."

"Who knows. You could have bought new glasses by that time, or they were trying out new technology. Listen, you have a good pedigree. You speak several languages. You're well travelled. You have no criminal record. They already suspect that you're one of us. What do you think? Do you have any interest?"

"I don't think so. Maybe. Let me think about it." The proposition might have possibilities.

"Okay. Hey, whatever happened to your Australian friend Jack Rielly? Is he back in Canada?"

"He married Jadwiga Bilecki and went back to Australia."

"Where they worry more about Chinese interference and espio-nage than Russian," Thomas said. "Well, good for them."

"I owe him a bachelor party. I was his best man. Could Hana Sato's assassin have had anything to do with Jadwiga's father's death?"

"Why do you ask?"

"Jadwiga thought she recognized him."

Thomas took his time answering. "Yes, quite likely, but it wouldn't help anyone to suggest that outside of this phone call. I would say give them my congratulations, but don't do that either."

Interpol issued an international arrest warrant for Artem Timofeyevich for the murder of Hana Sato. Laurent identified him from a virtual lineup as the man who entered John and Hana's cabin on the train. He was the same person whom Jack and I later encountered at the Hockey Hall of Fame. He arrived in Canada as

Roman Melnyk. His true identity was revealed by the investigative website Bellingcat.

Bellingcat claimed to have found his face in an open-source photograph in a yearbook of the Russian Far Eastern Military Academy. Artem Timofeyevich was also in a car insurance database as the owner of a Volvo registered to the GRU foreign intelligence agency on Khoroshevskoye Shosse in Moscow. Several residents of Timofeyevich's home town in Russia apparently confirmed his identity when shown images of him taken in Canada.

That Bellingcat could do this alone without input from a Western, three-letter intelligence service beggars belief. To me, it sounds like bullshit to make the Russians look amateurish and disguise the actual methods used to out Timofeyevich.

There was no arrest warrant for the second assassin. There was no clear image of his face to incriminate him. He was always crouched over with his eyes squeezed shut in video footage. No one was ever charged in the murder of John Hammersmith, aka Hartley.

Russian officials issued routine denials and offers of assistance in finding the real culprits. They proposed ludicrous alternative theories of Hana having been assassinated by Western intelligence agencies or Novichok being an unusual but natural by-product of human decomposition. An extradition request for Timofeyevich was denied under Article 61 of the Russian constitution, forbidding the extradition of Russian citizens.

Timofeyevich appeared on Russian television taking a lie detector test, which he passed with flying colours. One week later, Putin was photographed awarding Timofeyevich a medal of honour for "services to the motherland."

His penalty is that he can never leave the prison that is Russia. He can never visit Vancouver or San Francisco, Banff in the Rockies or Wengen in the Alps, never marvel at Spirit Island or Niagara Falls, never cycle along the canals in Coventry or Amsterdam, never go to the beach in Bayfield, Sopot or Sydney, never drink an espresso in Elora, Gdansk or Paris.

Scrolling through the text messages on my phone, I found the mystery text advising me not to quibble about who killed whom. The author was parading his knowledge of English grammar. Native English speakers don't say *whom*. I typed *Slava Ukraini* into the reply field and pressed send.

In the gym beside the weight room of the Coventry Rec Centre, the ballroom dance club was practicing the tango. The dancers were nowhere near the calibre of Hana and John. I was trying to remember the colour of the toothbrushes in their cabin on the train—if there was a pink and a blue one—and I believe that there was. Even thinking like the Russian FSB, there was no need to poison the pink toothbrush.

Postscriptum

Jack and I still exchange emails every few months. He sent me some pics of his do-over wedding to Jadwiga in Australia. It didn't look like it was as much fun as the first one. The images were stocked with smiling relatives, but there was no evident drama or spontaneity.

If I told you that Jadwiga repeated a year of residency training in Australia to become a licenced pediatrician, and during that year she became pregnant, you would think I was making it up for the sake of a good story. However, that's exactly what did happen.

Artem Timofeyevich was elected to serve as a member of the Russian parliament.

IF YOU ENJOYED THIS BOOK and would like to receive notification when the next in series becomes available, please go to www.petertinits.com and fill out the contact form. Click the Free Content tab and scroll to read previews of works in progress. Please also leave a review on Amazon and/or GoodReads.

MORE BOOKS by Peter Tinits

A CAUSE and MANNER: A sleep-deprived anesthesiologist consults his friends on dealing severely with his wife's lover. This first-in-series Matthias Kork novel, published in 2020, features suspense, dark humour and physicians behaving badly.

MILLENNIUM LAMENT: Rupi Kaur for your father—a collection of darkly humorous, illustrated poetry, published in 2022.

AN UNDETERMINED MANNER of DEATH: The attractive beneficiary of a new life insurance policy promotes a homicide verdict to the coroner investigating her father's apparent suicide. This second-in-series Matthias Kork novel, published in 2023, features a humorous blend of lying, killing and Mennonites.